A Beginner's Murder

Robert Strong

PROSPERO

Copyright © Robert Strong 1996

All rights reserved.

No part of this book may be reproduced by any means, nor transmitted, nor translated into a machine language, without the written permission of the publisher.

Prospero Books
46 West Street
Chichester
West Sussex
PO19 1RP

A CIP catalogue record for this book is available from the British Library.

ISBN 1 873475 22 5

Printed and bound in Great Britain.

Cover design by David Goodman.

For Estelle

A Beginner's Murder

Chapter 1

Richard Smith did not open his letters after his breakfast on the last day of the summer term. He stuffed them into the pocket of his sports jacket and left the dishes unwashed on the kitchen table of his bachelor flat. He was not looking forward to the last day of the school year. Mr Bender, the Head, would have the teachers spend the day with their own forms, "Good for personal relationships — a pastoral opportunity". 5 S's personal relationships tended to be vicious and the ministrations of a severe trainer of wild animals seemed, to their teacher, more appropriate than that of a shepherd. However, he reflected, as he sat in the inevitable traffic jam on the by-pass, at least he would not have to teach them. The less moronic would play cards and the others, the computer games they were allowed to bring in on the last day; he would be able to add up the columns of his register and tidy his desk. The day too, would be mercifully short for at 2.30 pm there would be the Final Assembly when Mr Bender would give them all his (strictly secular) blessing and a surprisingly large number of pupils leaving the school for the last time, would weep unashamedly, although they had hated the place from the first, vandalised it frequently and played truant as often as they dared.

Alderman Thomas Grimshaw Comprehensive, (formerly Alderman Grimshaw Grammar School), was firmly Progressive. Mr Bender believed devoutly in unstreamed classes, co-education, sex education and the role of the school in the process of social change. He did not believe, (and had had several letters on the subject published in the Guardian), in the publication of examination results. He also believed in Creative Writing, which is why he did not approve of Richard Smith, for that young man had once expressed the opinion at a Staff Meeting, that the phrase was another term for gibberish. The Head did most of the talking at Staff Meetings and no teacher who was interested in promotion, ever expressed anti- progressive opinions. It was another thing about Richard Smith that irritated Mr Bender. He never seemed keen on advancement. The Head would have tried to get rid of him but for the fact that he was an exceptionally good teacher of English Literature. Even Mr Bender had to consider the matter of 'A' Level results. If the middle-class families of the western suburbs of Bridgeminster were to continue to send their children to Grimshaw, there had to be some successes and Smith's classes tended to produce more grade A's than those of any other teacher. This undoubted fact had persuaded Mr Bender to tolerate Richard Smith's choice of set books, retaining Shakespeare, Chaucer and (horror of horrors), even Tennyson, and whenever possible, rejecting the more disgusting modern novels. He had even got away with refusing to use 'Lord of the Flies'.

The reader will have guessed that Richard Smith was a thoroughly conservative young man and the well-worn sports jacket with the collar and tie , marked him out from his T-shirted fellow teachers, as did his refusal to permit his pupils to address him by his Christian name, (or "forename", as the Head would prefer). As Darren McGuire, of 4F, a master of creative writing, put it succinctly, "He's like my f—— Grandad," which was odd, as McGuire senior was a moderately unsuccessful burglar, who had spent many years in Her Majesty's Prisons; but he did also wear a tweed jacket.

Richard Smith was a shy man and particularly shy with the opposite sex. Not all the women teachers at Grimshaws were hard-faced feminists; "relationships" were common and occasionally even marriages. Richard Smith was not bad looking and on several occasions had been noticed favourably by temporarily unattached young women. As Dawn Parkin, (Religious Studies and Sex Education), observed to her friend Mary Bannerman, (Physical Education),

"It's no good. Nothing works with him. And it can't be because he's gay because George or Colin or Teddy would have got him by now. Or even Philip."

All this explains why, during mid-morning break, Richard Smith got out his letters while his colleagues discussed their holiday plans or expressed satisfaction that certain of the more repulsive pupils were finally leaving. The first letter was from his credit card company, the computer telling him that he had 0 pounds 0 pence to pay. The second reminded him that his subscription to the local Theatre Club was due. The third was an offer to give him the chance of winning thousands of pounds if he would subscribe to a well-known monthly magazine, against whose crudely summarised versions of the English classics Richard Smith frequently warned his 'A' Level pupils. The fourth letter was different. The address was printed by something vastly superior to an ordinary office typewriter and the paper was heavy and expensive. Moreover, it was addressed to Richard Smith Esquire, the combination of feudal rank and fine vellum, suggesting wealth and power. It did more. It came from Palgraves, Solicitors of Lincoln Inn Fields and told Richard Smith that he was to become rich. "Acting as agents for McCabe & Fraser, Attorneys of Melbourne, Australia, we have to inform you that we have been commissioned to discover your whereabouts and to inform you that you are the sole heir to the estate of your late uncle Sir Malcolm Smith Bart of River Bend, New South Wales, the will, made on October 10, 1992 and submitted to probate by," etc etc. "We are informed that the value of the estate is very large, certainly many millions of Australian dollars."

The letter went on to express the hope that Sir Richard, (as he would become when proof of his identity could be submitted), would be so good as to call on the writer, (a Mr Pickford, Senior Partner) at his earliest convenience to discuss the matter.

Now some young men receiving this letter would have leapt to their feet and danced for joy. Not Richard Smith. His first thought was literary; "Pure H G Wells", and he thought of Kipps in the drapery emporium. The second thought was of young Martin Edgeworth of Upper 6th. Edgeworth was leaving today and in 4 or 5 weeks would certainly learn that he had failed his 'A' Levels. A few weeks before, Richard Smith had told the class something about the Tichborne case and the missing heir, (oddly enough it came up in a lesson on Trollope). Edgeworth had been interested in the subject and, unusually for him, even asked questions. Edgeworth's father was a printer. True the letter was not in the boy's usual sub-literate style but his friend Butterfield's father was a solicitor. "After all," Smith reflected, "an end-of-year joke is quite traditional. Surprising they had the energy though."

He read through the letter again and reflected. "It must be a joke — Sir Richard indeed! Now, that is over the top! And anyway,

I haven't got an Uncle Malcolm — no uncle at all in fact. Still, I must show Edgeworth I'm not so easily tricked." He got out of the battered armchair provided by the local authority for the comfort of the staff and made his way down the corridor to the entrance hall, observing as he passed that the good old tradition of drinking cider and lager on the last day of term, was being extended to ever younger pupils each year. In the entrance hall there was a telephone for the use of staff only. Richard Smith asked for Directory Enquiries and demanded the number of Palgraves, of Lincoln Inn Fields, Solicitors. To his surprise, it was the number on the letterhead. "The little devils have been thorough," he reflected. He dialled the London number. An incredibly well - spoken young woman replied. Could he speak to Mr Pickford? Mr Pickford was with a client. Could he speak to anybody? Mr Gaiford might be free — what was the business? Richard told her. Yes, she had heard of the matter. Mr Gaiford would know.

Mr Gaiford's voice was old; very old. He was Senior Clerk, much too grand to think of calling himself a Legal Executive. Richard Smith was very impressed as the venerable lawyer explained that he had not had any personal concern in Sir Richard's matter, but he understood that Mr Pickford was anxious to meet Sir Richard and if Sir Richard, etc etc. He went on slowly, his congratulations to the new baronet taking so long that that slightly stunned armiger had to fumble in his pockets for more coins.

So it was true! Richard Smith's reaction was perhaps surprising. He congratulated himself on never really believing that Edgeworth and Butterfield were up to such a well-constructed hoax. Richard Smith would like to believe that he could unmask any literary forgery.

His further thoughts became rather confused. 'Many millions of Australian dollars.' How much was an Australian dollar? Was it like a franc or the American kind? As he walked back to the staff-room, the bell rang for classes and he altered course for his own classroom. 5 S were drifting back and none of them looked dangerously inebriated. Smith opened his 'Telegraph' and satisfied himself as to the value of the dollar. It was not, he was pleased to see, like the franc. It must be millions of pounds. What does a man do with millions? 5 S had already sensed that their form master's thoughts were on other things. The noise had become louder than was permissible even on the last day of term.

Emerging from his reverie to shout at them, he reflected that what a man does not do when he is rich is — teach. Richard had often faced grimly the prospect of another 32 years at the blackboard but now —? What sort of income does a million pounds, say, produce? He did a quick sum on his blotter. Do millionaires pay more tax? He rather thought they did. Mathematics was never his subject. What do you do with millions?

Conservatives are not often optimists by nature. Before the classroom din became again intolerable, Richard Smith had another thought. After all, 'Richard Smith' is a common name. They must have got hold of the wrong one! That would account for it! People do not get left millions today by uncles in Australia. You could not write a novel with such a device in the plot. Perhaps in television soap operas? Richard Smith did not watch TV much. And how could a man have an uncle-baronet and not know about it? That thought, however, led to another. How much did he know about his father's family? Richard Smith was from a broken home, told as a child that his father had 'gone away' and, never succeeding to get his mother to say much about him. An only child, he had been adequately looked after, her salary as a district nurse providing them both with reasonable comfort, but she had few friends and her two sisters in Yorkshire were the only relatives he knew of. He always believed that he loved his mother but in her words they had 'never been close'. She had died of cancer during his final year at university and his tutor had attributed to his loss the fact that he received a good Second instead of the hoped-for First.

In such musings did Richard Smith get through the last day of term enduring the hearty farewells of 5S and the dreary platitudes of the Headmaster. It was a Wednesday.

On the Thursday morning Richard Smith parked his Ford Fiesta in the station car park and took the train for London. Palgrave's offices, (or did one call them Chambers?), in Lincoln's Inn fields, were as impressive as the receptionist's telephone voice. Georgian, spacious, carpeted and obviously expensively furnished, with original paintings and engravings on the waiting-room walls. He did not have to wait long.

Mr Pickford was large, handsome and elegantly dressed, with what Richard rather thought was an Old Etonian tie. There had been only one old Etonian at his not-very-fashionable Oxford college. Richard Smith felt nervous at first sight of this very impressive figure. Where had he read that old-fashioned solicitors offer dry sherry from precious cut-glass decanters to their clients? A glass of sherry might steady his nerves. However, it all went very smoothly. "We have, of course, made all the necessary enquiries and satisfied ourselves as to your identity. I must however, ask you to confirm the facts we have uncovered. What was your father's name?"

"Edmund Smith, born somewhere in Lancashire, Manchester I believe I was told."

"Quite so, quite so; and your mother?"

"She was born Emma Cornthwaite in Huddersfield. I believe that her parents kept a shop there. I never knew them."

"You have, I suppose, your own and your mother's birth certificates, marriage lines and so on."

"Yes, I have brought them along."

"Of course, of course — purely a formality," said the lawyer, glancing at the creased documents that Richard Smith produced from an old envelope. "All you have said confirms what we have already discovered. I congratulate you, Sir Richard, on your inheritance."

"But, but — are you quite sure? Could there be some mistake? I didn't even know I had an uncle, let alone a baronet, and rich, too. How did he get to know about me?"

Mr Pickford leaned back in his handsome chair and smiled across his clearly priceless antique desk. Now that the inheritance was confirmed he was perfectly prepared to spend quite a long time with a rich client. "I have a letter here from your late uncle's Australian solicitor. I will let you have a copy of it. Your uncle inherited the title from his father, your grandfather, who received it for — er- political services, during Lloyd George's government in the 1920's. He died in 1942 in reduced circumstances, in fact, bankrupt and the title passed to his eldest son, your late uncle then serving as a Lance Corporal in the Army Catering Service. He did not use the title and in 1948 emigrated to Australia where he lived until his death last March."

"How did he become rich?"

"Meat pies. Well, meat pies at first," said the solicitor with evident distaste. "Meat pies, sausages, black puddings and, what are, I believe, known as 'fast foods'. His products are known throughout the Antipodes but he diversified, as they say, into a variety of enterprises. He also invested heavily and successfully, in Australian mining and transport."

Richard Smith's next question was, "Did he ever marry?"

"No. I understand that there were one or two rather brief relationships, and there was, so Mr McCabe says, the possibility of a claim by a young woman who lived with him for a while, but nothing serious." Richard Smith digested all this for a long moment which moved Mr Pickford to glance at the very handsome clock on his mantelpiece. "You said that the estate was large — in fact, I think — millions."

"Oh yes, many millions," said the solicitor in the solemn voice he used when speaking of wealth. "McCabes say that when death duties, which are as extortionate in Australia as in this unfortunate island, are paid, you should receive something between thirty and fifty million. It may be much more."

Richard Smith gulped. "Dollars?" he whispered. "Oh no, pounds. A very comfortable inheritance, Sir Richard."

The solicitor was obviously thinking of his next client and Richard Smith moved to leave. "We can, of course, arrange an advance of any sum you might require." Mr Pickford had already assessed the quality of Richard's only dark suit — Marks & Spencer, ready-made and excellent value at seventy pounds and his shoes also the product of St Michael.

"It will take some months to wind up the estate and of course, you will need to spend money with your new responsibilities."

The alarming word 'responsibilities' almost induced panic in the teacher's heart. Millions and responsibilities." No thank you, Mr Pickford. I think I had better get used to the idea first.

But, can we keep all this quiet. I wouldn't want it talked about — not yet, anyway."

"We of course observe the strictest confidentiality," murmured the lawyer. The Press however, do seem to have ways of finding out about things. And the title, of course, that can hardly be kept secret."

"Can't one renounce it, like Wedgwood Benn?"

"Not a baronetcy, I fancy. The point has never been raised, to my knowledge. Of course, you need not use it. And you must consider your heirs." That was another alarming thought. Baronets had heirs. It was clearly time to leave.

Richard Smith took the 2.30 pm train back to Bridgeminster in a strangely subdued state of mind. It was not so much the money. He had money. In his own estimation he was already quite rich. His mother had left him her (admittedly mortgaged) semi-detached house. He had inherited almost £50,000 and had bought his flat for £30,000. He had, he remembered, over £20,000 in a deposit account and some Unit Trusts. He had no mortgage and was never overdrawn. Even his five-year old Fiesta was bought for cash. Did he need millions?

Then, the title. He had known one or two men at Oxford who had titles. Some were Honourables. They were much like other fellows but usually drank more. Nobody at his college used their titles but Mr Pickford and his staff had 'Sir Richarded' him continually. It was very odd. Then the thought crossed his mind. "I made the pupils call me 'Sir'. Should they call me Sir Richard now?" And that thought led to another. He need not teach any longer. He could be free!

The new baronet's thoughts so occupied his mind that he almost forgot to get off the train at Bridgeminster. He reached his car and found that it had been broken into and the radio stolen. He was about to be conventionally outraged when he reflected. "What did it really matter? You can buy any amount of radios with millions. Or cars." He did not bother to report the theft at the police station.

Chapter 2

Richard's hopes of keeping the news of his inheritance secret were, of course, dashed. Miss Kendrick, secretary to the junior partner at Venables saw to that. Palgraves dealt mainly with rich and/or notorious clients and she had an arrangement with a young journalist with whom she was intimate. His paper's editor was rather pleased with the headline, "Sir, becomes Sir Richard" but even that baronet's 'Daily Telegraph' carried the story on an inner page, with rather more detail about the meat-pie fortune and the true reasons for the creation of the title by the Welsh Wizard.

Then came the letters. Sacks of letters, mostly begging for money, although some pleaded support for a remarkable range of lost causes. There were letters offering a seat on a board of companies he had never heard of, (and some he had) and others offered him the opportunity to make vast sums of money by the safest of investments. He wondered why anyone should think that a man with millions would want to speculate. It was a sobering thought.

There were also proposals of marriage. It was necessary to escape. The first escape was by joining a cultural tour of Hungary organised by the Educational Opportunities Trust. It sounded exciting and in a way it was. The leader, a bearded left-wing artist named Sheepstone, was accompanied by his wife and two badly-behaved children. They travelled free but the other members, mainly retired bank clerks and local government officers, paid through the nose. There were extras. Sheepstone, too, did not make things easy. He misjudged the time that every journey should take so that they always got back to their hotel late and the surly staff, (who had not recovered from their Communist Training), served them with a cold and disagreeable meal. The leader had also failed to do his homework: several museums he had planned to include in the tour were closed for repair and the hotels chosen were universally dire. Sheepstone, who, with Marxist fervour, hated royalty, the church and the aristocracy equally, took every opportunity to insult his titled passenger. Richard had of course, failed to remain incognito. His picture had appeared in too many illustrated papers. On the fifth day, he abandoned the tour and returned to England. A notice on the door of his flat told him that the Post Office had found it impossible to deliver any more mail and would he please collect it from the Sorting Office. It was indeed difficult to pass through the hallway.

Now the problem was the telephone. His number had always been ex-directory but now it had become known. The telephone beggars usually ended by becoming abusive. After three days, he called the travel agents, found that a round-the-world cruise had a vacant berth and that the 'Ocean Gem' would sail in six days' time. It was fantastically expensive but Palgraves had already transferred huge sums of money to his bank, the manager of which had never seen such a large credit entry in a current account. The travel agent had murmured something about the Captain's Table and dinner jackets. Richard Smith had never owned such a garment, though he had once hired one for the ball after Final Schools. Still, Moss Bros had fixed him up with a ready-made suit and an hour or two of practising the making of a bow-tie, had made him reasonably proficient. On a cold, wet Thursday in autumn he sailed from Southampton.

Of his seventy five days at sea it is not necessary to say much. He was not sea-sick and after the first week got quite used to the dinner jacket. The passengers were all elderly, rich and boring and talked most freely about their ailments, even the embarrassing symptoms. One passenger only, provided Sir Richard with interesting conversation. Father Randall had been sent on the cruise by his loving parishioners after a major operation. He did not want to come but thought it uncharitable to refuse this generous gift. He was small, thin, of ascetic appearance and spent a large part of each day immersed in theological works. Richard had thought he was of the Roman persuasion, but was later surprised to learn that he had been married and had five children. His wife was dead. Richard, mildly agnostic, found himself arguing about religion with the ardent Anglo-Catholic. Sometimes they were joined by Mr Benbow, the ship's official chaplain, a hearty evangelical who despised Father Randall and all his works. On the whole, Father Randall, (Balliol 1939-42), got the better of the arguments. During the last few days of the cruise, Richard told the priest about his fortune.

"What should I do?" he asked.

The priest leaned back in his deckchair. "One gets asked for advice but I have never had your problem put to me before. I don't think I'm competent. But, I say this not as a priest, you should ask yourself, 'What do I really want?' Not much help, I'm afraid. Time for another of the Captain's monologues." The Captain of the 'Ocean Gem' was famous for his repertoire of sea stories, mostly untrue, and they went down to dinner.

Sir Richard Smith returned to his bachelor flat on a cold November day. The flood of mail had abated but there were a number of really pathetic appeals. As he sat before his electric fire he asked himself again; what did he really want to do? They had let him resign his post at the school without the normal notice; Mr Bender had been most agreeable and the staff had given him a set of sherry glasses.

He did not regret giving up teaching but he knew he was going to be bored. Was he, he wondered, the only man in England who did not want most of the things that money can buy? He discovered that on the third day of his affluence when he passed Rutters Garage and looked at the Mercedes cars in their showroom. He could buy a Mercedes, if it would go into his garage, but what was wrong with his Fiesta? The watches in Spink's window at £500 did not appeal either, his £10 Japanese timepiece was perfectly accurate. He rather thought he might buy some new clothes. But what was he to do? What had the shabby little clergyman said, "What do you really want?"

He did know what he wanted although he hardly permitted the thought to enter his conscious mind. Richard Smith had an obsession that he revealed to no-one. He had two libraries. The bookcases in his sitting-room were filled with cheap editions of the English classics and the books used for his degree course but the books on the shelves in his bedroom were all detective-fiction, Conan-Doyle, Dorothy Sayers, Christie, Simenon; they were all there. He read and re-read them. Once a Mastermind contestant had scored 16 points on the Poirot books. Richard Smith had known all the answers. He did not read American detective stories much. It was the elegant, cultured, slightly eccentric English amateur that appealed to him; Lord Peter, Max Carrados, Sir Henry Merrivale. In fantasy he saw himself in such a life. Then the thought emerged, "Why not?"

Now, Sir Richard Smith Bart was no fool. He realised that crimes do not conveniently take place whenever an amateur detective is available. There are no villages like that of Miss Marples. But, there was crime. Among his acquaintances was Detective Sergeant Polk, a member of the Bridgeminster Theatre Club and a popular one too, still just young enough for the role of juvenile lead. (Richard, of course, did not act but was a reliable prompter and backstage man.) Polk sometimes discussed local cases but the general impression the policeman gave was that the Force always knew which of the local villains had committed the crime but were frequently frustrated by the tricks of lawyers, for which profession the Sergeant had no great liking. He must talk to Polk.

Then, the thought came. All detectives have to have an assistant; a Watson, a Bunter, a Hastings. In all his life Smith had never given an order to anyone over the age of 18.

The thought of employing an assistant was frightening. But then Holmes had solved cases before the Doctor entered 221B, Baker Street. That problem could be solved later.

For the next few weeks, Sir Richard looked at crimes. The Millbank Road Post Office was held up and £10,000 due to be paid out to old-age pensioners taken. Richard was there the next day and even got to talk to Mrs Hampton, the postmaster's wife. She told him nothing significant except that the robbers had had 'evil eyes', and that the police had been lovely. Next, there was a series of sexual assaults on children in the local park. Somehow, this did not seem the right sort of crime. One day he drove to Portborough, the radio having told him of a multiple killing in a back street. By the time he arrived, the crowd was dispersing; "They got him, mate. Ugly devil too. Took four coppers to get him in the van. Escaped from the loony-bin, they say." Mad criminals are only interesting to psychiatrists.

Then Mrs Sellars in the flat below was burgled. It was, of course, her own fault. She had left her door unlocked to go to the corner shop and returned to find the more saleable of her possessions missing. Richard knew the lady slightly — a grey-haired but sprightly widow who, it was said, had had theatrical connections at some time in her life. She had called to congratulate him when he had inherited his fortune, and, as she admitted to her friend, Diane Sharp, found him fascinating. "A real baronet you know, and with the manners to go with it. A proper nobleman though as shy as a kitten." She further expressed the regret that she was not twenty years younger when she would have liked to have had the chance to "make a man of him".

Richard heard of the burglary on the following day. The milkman told him the news as he collected the weekly milk money. (In spite of his millions now accumulating at an impressive rate, Sir Richard distrusted monthly accounts). Indeed, Henry the milkman was somewhat indignant at the questioning he had endured from a bored Detective Constable who had already visited the scene of eight similar break-ins that week, and who knew very well that there was only the smallest chance that the thieves would be caught.

"Asked me if I knew that the lady left her door on the latch. And wanted to know when I finished my round yesterday. Me, who's been doing this job since I left school and never wrong in my books at the end of the week!" The angry milkman received soothing words and departed with a clatter of empty bottles and Richard, carefully locking his front door, took the staircase to the two flats below. Mrs Sellars was Number Two.

"I've come to offer my sympathy, Mrs Sellars. I've just heard of your nasty experience." Mrs Sellars had opened the door clad in a housecoat patterned with flowers by a surrealist artist. "Oh Sir Richard, how kind of you. Do come in. Have you had your tea? The kettle is on — they left me my kettle!"

"Did they steal very much?"

"My TV and record player and my silver spoons, not many of them I'm afraid. And the cup my husband won for snooker only I don't think it was real silver you know. They took my bits of jewellery although they weren't worth very much. It's really all the mess they made and everything thrown about. At least I'm insured though, through General Provincial."

Mrs Sellars did not seem over-distressed. She explained that a nice young lady had called to give her counselling.

"May I just look around? I'm — er- interested in er- crime, you see."

"Of course. I'll go and make the tea."

"Mrs Lummus was saying only the other day that in your new position you ought to be on the Bench." Richard was used to people telling him things he ought to be doing in his new position.

The flat had been tidied up. Only the empty stands for the TV and record player told of the burglary. What did a detective do in this sort of case? The police would naturally look for finger prints but what else could one do? He looked round. Curtains with more violent flowers, a hideous standard lamp, a small bookcase with paper backs, a china clock...... He glanced in at the bedroom door but did not like to enter. The bathroom had been entered and a medicine cabinet had been pulled off the wall. Mrs Sellars summoned him to take tea. "Did the police look for fingerprints?" he asked.

"They puffed their powder all over the place — windows, door knobs, everywhere, but I don't think they found anything." He sipped his tea. He disliked Earl Grey intensely but he guessed that Mrs Sellars had been watching an extremely persuasive TV commercial which, filmed in some of England's stateliest homes, implied that the rich, (and titled), invariably consumed that brand. "They say they only solve about one tenth of break-ins like this, but they caught the men who cleared out the off-licence last month." 'So they should,' thought Richard. 'They overloaded the van they used so that it broke an axle on the motorway.' He looked around the room as she prattled on. Probably the most stupid criminal would know about fingerprints and wear gloves or wipe the door-knob or .... As he mused, his attention was caught by a small white object lying in the fireplace. It was, as one might have expected, a matchstick, except that no fire was ever lit in Mrs Sellars' centrally heated flat.

It was no ordinary matchstick for it had been bent by a series of cracks, into a half-circle. He put down his unpleasant cup of tea and picked up the object. "Oh dear, how untidy the place gets. It must have been that policeman but he wasn't smoking on duty, I will say that for him and very polite I'm sure." Richard Smith was thinking. Where had he seen matchsticks bent into shapes like that? Somebody's funny little habit. Now, wait a minute! Mrs Sellars chatted happily about policeman and what her late husband thought about them, but now Richard had remembered.

"Mrs Sellars," he said, "Do you think I might use your telephone?" She took him into the hall, where he glanced through her directory and dialled a number. "Bridgeminster police station? May I speak to Detective Sergeant Polk?" There was quite a delay but eventually the deep over-theatrical voice of James Polk, (fresh from the role of Ernest in the Theatre Club's triumphant production of Wilde's masterpiece), was heard. "Richard Smith here. Jim, I'm speaking from the flat of Mrs Christine Sellars, my neighbour. She was burgled yesterday."

"Hello Richard. Spent the millions yet? The police sports fund would welcome a contribution! I hear you're getting proposals of marriage in every post!" (Polk's heavy humour was well-known.)

"No, just listen a minute Jim. If you talk to Gary Crosley, now aged about nineteen and living somewhere on the Uplands estate, Glanville Road, I think, you'll probably find that he knows something about it. He's tall, weedy and spotty — or he was when he was in Four F."

"Oh we know his family, all right. Never had anything on him except a breach of the peace now and again. Not that there is ever much peace on that estate! How do you know anyway?"

"Never mind 'how', for the moment. Just say 'information received'."

"Well, if you say so. Soon check up. What did you think of the play?" The detective would have liked to have gone on talking theatre during working hours, but Richard persuaded him to get on with the job. Mrs Sellars had of course heard every word spoken by her guest. "How did you know, Sir Richard? Will I get my things back? It sounds like a miracle."

"Well actually, it is rather odd but I'd better not say anything until they make sure, but it was this matchstick. Have you an envelope to put it in?"

In the best professional manner, Richard sealed the pale mauve envelope which the lady had provided, writing on it, 'Found in fireplace of Flat 2, Downview Mansions." He added the date and signed it. "You should sign too, Mrs Sellars." Mrs Sellars' hand shook with pure excitement as she added her name. "Oh you are clever, Sir Richard," she murmured and as she saw him out wished again that she was twenty, (or actually thirty) years younger.

That evening as Richard Smith sat before his electric fire re-reading 'Gaudy Night,' for perhaps the tenth time, his door bell rang. Sergeant Polk sank gratefully into the new easy chair on which the baronet had recently spent no less than £150 of his fortune. He accepted a whisky, for Richard now kept a variety of drinks in his cupboard although he still preferred Sainsbury's medium dry sherry for himself.

"What I want to know is, how did you know it was young Gary? We found the whole lot in his dad's garden shed, and a lot of other stuff that's been nicked. He says that he wants twenty or thirty other cases taken into consideration. The 'Super's' very pleased. How did you catch on?"

Richard was modest enough to blush. "Well, it was just a chance. You see, I used to teach Gary and I remember that he has this odd habit of bending matchsticks and leaving them about. I remember because I thought at the time it was odd that a layabout like him should have neurotic habits. But of course, it's an egalitarian age!"

Polk was not quite sure what 'egalitarian' meant but let it pass. "We used to make him pick them up and put them in his pocket. I've been thinking that when he took out his handkerchief to wipe off the fingerprints he made on the mantelpiece, one of them must have fallen out. Here's the matchstick." He handed Polk the envelope.

"Well we won't really need evidence. He's made a full statement. Lucky you remembered though. I thought for a moment that you'd done some real detecting. Nice whisky, this."

Sir Richard poured him another and had to endure another half hour of theatrical reminiscences and gossip about the private affairs of members of the Theatre Club.

Chapter 3

The reader must not think that Smith's First Case turned that would-be detective's head. It was not, he realised, proper detection. It caused him acute embarrassment, for again the Press got hold of the news. This time it was the work of a very senior constable (with no hope of promotion), who for years had supplemented his income by passing tit-bits on to the local paper. "Millionaire Baronet Solves Crime", the press announced, after Gary had been put on probation for twelve months by a kindly magistrate, who spoke sympathetically of the social deprivation he had suffered. It might have cost him more than embarrassment too, for some mates of Gary threw stones at his windows one dark night. Fortunately, they chose the wrong windows and smashed those of Mr Henry Mordaunt, a retired undertaker, who occupied number seven; causing damage to the extent of £350.75p.

The publicity and the irritating behaviour of various acquaintances who now addressed him as "Sir Sherlock", or even "Lord Peter, I presume?!", led him to yet another attempt to escape. This time it was a railway journey across Russia and a cruise in Eastern waters: fantastically expensive but proving quite enjoyable. He was not so keen on railways as he was on detection but the journey across the endless Steppes was fascinating and by the end of it he had acquired an unexpected taste for caviar. There was no murder for him though on the Moscow express!

Bridgeminster had changed little when he returned. His bank had written again about the vast sums accumulating in his current account and suggesting that he should avail himself of the services of their "financial consultant". He supposed that he would have to do something about it and actually sent a large cheque to Father Randall, the priest who had sat next to him on the boat deck of the Ocean Gem. He remembered that the clergyman had said something about a new church roof. How much did a new church roof cost? He sent £20,000, which his bank manager noted, did little to reduce that overflowing balance.

So life passed at Bridgeminster. In December, the Theatre Club presented "Blithe Spirit", another triumph for James Polk as the husband and Richard was busy as assistant stage manager. Polk's wife, bored with his long absences at rehearsals, began a much discussed affair with Detective Constable Bosworth, her husband's colleague. The force, after all, is a close-knit body.

Christmas passed. Richard sent extravagant presents to his Yorkshire aunts, put on his dinner jacket for the theatre club's annual 'do', and spent a long weekend as the guest of Father Randall who, overawed by the munificent gift, had invited him to his lonely vicarage. Richard, remembering that in spite of his ascetic appearance the priest had shown a remarkable capacity for the vintage wines provided by the stewards of the Ocean Gem, took with him a suitably filled hamper. The visit was more enjoyable than he expected. The widower-priest had no housekeeper, the huge rectory was not well heated and the bed rather damp but his conversation was lively and his reminiscences of the Oxford of his day amusing.

Richard overcame his agnostic prejudices so far as to attend Evensong at his host's church, a gloomy red-brick, Gothic pile, not too well-attended, but with an excellent choir. Richard was pleased that they still used the Book of Common Prayer. "But only at Evensong, I'm afraid," said the Rector. "There is a Progressive element to consider."

That Sunday evening, they sat before the rector's fire, finishing the second bottle of the vintage port that his guest had provided. Two glasses was the ex-teacher's normal limit; the priest's capacity seemed infinite and Richard had felt obliged to take more than his usual share. It moved him to talk more freely than usual.

"Have you decided on a new career?" asked the priest. "I remember asking you if you knew what you really wanted. I suppose that everything is open to you now? You could read for the Bar, or perhaps politics, or... did you say that you were keen on the theatre? You could even buy one, you know. I think they call them "angels"! Pity about your lack of faith. There are so few rich men in Holy Orders nowadays. They'd make you a Canon of Westminster, or something like that, in no time." Father Randall was very cynical about the authorities of the Established Church.

Now whether it was the extra glasses of port combined with the heat of the fire and the large and badly-cooked meal which his host had provided, it is impossible to say, but Sir Richard Smith Bart was moved to tell the priest of his secret ambition. To his surprise he was not laughed at. "But this was my own -well, fantasy I suppose, years ago. The Father Brown stories, you know. Have you read them?" Richard knew them by heart. "I am sure that God will give you the opportunity." (Father Randall had a most embarrassing way of bringing God into the conversation.) "I shall make a special mention for your hopes in my prayers. Not that I shall pray for a crime to be committed for you, of course, but if crimes there must be, that you should have the opportunity of investigating them. Do have another glass of this excellent port, my dear boy." Wine made Father Randall sound rather like a stage vicar!

The reader must not think that Richard was converted to a belief in the power of prayer by the events of the week following his visit, but he certainly remembered the rector's words.

Chapter 4

Sir Richard Smith was now on the committee of the Theatre Club. They had insisted on that and his first contribution to the funds had delighted the Honorary Treasurer. The business of the meeting on the 20th January concerned the choice of the next production. A faction wanted "Look Back in Anger" but the treasurer had argued persuasively that it would not be "box office" in Bridgeminster! The faction had looked hopefully at Richard; perhaps he might be persuaded to finance the show? Richard ignored the hints. He preferred light, romantic comedies and gave his vote for 'Hobson's Choice'.

'Hobson's Choice' was chosen. After the meeting, the committee retired to the Castle Inn where Richard found that they all thought it perfectly natural for him to buy the first round of drinks.

Sergeant Polk was in great spirits being perfectly confident that the casting committee would give him the role of Willy Glossop. He was also not going to let Richard forget what he wittily called 'The Case of the Bent Matchstick'.

Richard was quite used to such jokes. "Now what you want is a really good murder. Not a back street bashing. A toff shot in a locked library, cyanide in the champagne…. Sir Richard investigates! The Force completely baffled naturally!" The policeman enjoyed his own joke. It was a jolly end to the evening.

The 21st January was a cold day. Although the wind had shifted to the west and the thin covering of snow had disappeared, it was raw and damp. Harry Marder, the park keeper of the Abbey Gardens, left his cottage outside the park to open the ornate Victorian cast-iron gates, which had somehow escaped the wartime campaign to turn all such relics into guns and tanks. Harry was near retirement and not too keen on the morning inspection of his charge as laid down in his standing orders.

The Abbey Gardens are delightful in high summer. In winter they are not. Shaded by mature evergreen oaks and cedars, the place was dark and gloomy. In one corner of the park are the walls and arches that are all that remain of Bridgeminster Abbey. Harry pulled his uniform cap firmly down, turned up the collar of his coat and plodded on. The park is quite small. It would take him ten minutes at most to make the circuit and that would be his morning's work. Nobody would visit the park on such a day; he could sit by the fire until his official lunch-break when he would retire to the Abbey Tavern. It was a hard life, he reflected.

Passing the ruins, Harry saw something ahead of him on the path. His old eyes were not so good as they had been. A bundle or something? Those boys throwing things over the wall again? No, too far for that! He stooped over it. It was a dead man! The hands and feet were tied with what looked like clothes line. The body lay on its back. No doubt it was dead.

Now it was an odd fact but in all his sixty-one years Harry Marder had never seen a dead body. "Only on telly," he said afterwards to his wife. Quite clearly, he panicked. Stumbling on the gravel, he almost ran back the way he had come until he reached his home. His wife was washing the breakfast dishes morosely. "A dead man in the park!" She stared at him uncomprehending. "A dead man, I tell you — murdered! Dead and cold; frozen!" She still did not grasp it. "They won't like that at the office. Hadn't you better tell Mr Garrowby? Mr Garrowby was the universally disliked supervisor of Parks and the terror of the manual workers in the gardens. "It's a police matter woman," shouted her husband. "Let me get to the 'phone. This is a nine, nine, nine call."

Bridgeminster police had had mysterious deaths in the past but nothing like the Park Mystery as the locals came to call it — a domestic killing about once every five years and the still unsolved death of an American tourist found stabbed in his room at the Glendale Country Hotel and believed by the more imaginative to have been the victim of a revenge killing by the Mafia. But this killing certainly stimulated the local CID to activity. Within minutes Superintendent Garrett, Inspector Morris and Sergeant Polk were being led to the scene by a still-shaken park keeper fortified however, by a very stiff brandy, "for medicinal reasons", as he explained to his wife. The three detectives looked down at the corpse. "Know him, George?" asked the Super. "No sir. Don't think so. Face is very distorted. Nasty business. What about you, Jim?" Polk studied the body. "Yes sir, I fancy I've seen him —

somewhere. Local, I think. Can't put a name to him though. Respectable appearance sir."

The body was dressed in a well-cut grey suit. A regimental tie was visible and an expensive -looking watch, still going, was on the left wrist. The shoes were highly polished. "Better get all the lads along — photographer, surgeon and a bit of tent over him. All the police constables at the station will be needed to go over the ground as well. Get the park gates closed. Murder. No admittance to the public until further notice."

Polk, knowing that it was his job to get all this organised, left the group round the body. It gave him great satisfaction to think that a dozen young constables would have to leave the 'paperwork' they so much preferred to walking the beat and instead, spend hours crawling about a freezing park. But, that was life!

The body was quickly identified. Polk was right. It was a local man. None other than that of Colonel Maurice Wainwright, DSO,OBE, retired, Chairman of the District Council, aged seventy-two years and resident in the Bridgeminster area since leaving the army. The DSO had been won as a very young officer in the Korean War. His army career had otherwise been undistinguished. His face was indeed distorted, but Polk should have recognised him. For many years he had served on the local Bench. On reaching retirement age he had got himself elected, (in the Conservative interest), to the District Council. The Superintendent had heard that he was not altogether popular among the other Councillors. He was married, with two grown-up sons, both of whom were following their father in undistinguished careers in the army.

"And who would want to kill him — I can't imagine?" the Superintendent pondered. "It would be him. He gave us quite a lot of trouble a few years back. All those letters in the papers criticising the Force. What was it all about, George? Breathalising?"

"No sir, police corruption. Masonic influences in promotion, that sort of thing. The Chief Constable was very upset about it."

"Well he would be, wouldn't he?" The Super was not a Freemason.

"Yes, I remember now — I was off duty when it blew up. That was when I had my shingles." Superintendent Garrett had had quite a lot of time off duty due to sickness but never quite enough to persuade his superiors to suggest early retirement. It required sound judgement!

The three officers studied the police surgeon's report. The Colonel had been dead for up to twenty four hours. Death had been caused by a heavy blow to the back of the head which had caused a fracture of the skull. The dead man had not been robbed, his wallet containing £55 in notes. He carried a gold fountain pen and his expensive wristwatch, had not been taken.

"He wasn't one of those?" asked Morris, cryptically. "It's in the park where we're always picking them up."

"What, after dark, on a January night and snowing?" argued the Super. "Besides, it's coming back to me now. He wasn't that type. I can always spot them. Now, if you had mentioned the Admiral ...." The Superintendent referred to another local retired officer who had indeed been known, during his years afloat, as "Fanny".

The three detectives continued to ponder.

"Well, let's get on with it," ordered Garrett, meaning of course, that his subordinates should get on. "Widow, bank manager, solicitor — better see his doctor too. Who saw him last? All the usual stuff. And try to look a bit more cheerful Polk. You did that comic detective in one of your play-acting things in the Coronation Hall. I saw you — seats at £3, I remember. Cor."

Bank manager, solicitor and doctor were interviewed that afternoon, each of the three visibly excited by losing a customer, client and patient in such sensational circumstances. His bank account was in order — a healthy balance on deposit, a private income from sound investments plus the generous index-linked pension that Her Majesty grants even her less competent officers.

The solicitor had nothing to tell the Police. The Will was in order. The Colonel had never been involved in serious litigation.

"Any trouble with women or ...." murmured Polk.

"Good heavens no. Of course not," said Mr Trubshaw, (of Trubshaw, Trubshaw & Hackett). "A most moral man, the Colonel. Churchwarden you know." Polk had known churchwardens with very interesting tastes but he said nothing and took his leave. The doctor, though secretive as they always were, gave a similar story. There was nothing in the Colonel's medical history to interest the police. No drug-taking, no alcoholism, (although he liked a few drinks): nothing.

Inspector Morris interviewed the widow. The Wainwrights had occupied a charming cottage in the village of Hangleton about six miles from Bridgeminster. Mrs Wainwright had taken the shock of the murder well. Inspector Morris was inclined to think that her calmness indicated an unfeeling nature but the Inspector was wrong. Mrs Wainwright had married the then Captain Wainwright at the age of eighteen. She was herself from an army family and had spent most of her life in married quarters, seeing her husband off to minor wars from time to time:- Korea, Suez, Malaya, Aden. It was not easy to shock her now.

She had last seen her husband at breakfast on the day of his death. He had had a letter from his stockbroker in London and he told her that he would have to go up to town to see the man. "Stupid fellow", he had said. "Can't get the simplest instructions carried out. Catch the 11.10." She had driven him to the station, "as we only have one car now."

"Hadn't she been worried when her husband hadn't returned?"

"No not really. He occasionally stayed the night at his club. He kept some things there in his locker. He didn't get the chance to see his old army friends very often. I expect he would have rung up to tell me but I was out most of the day. It was the WI party night." (Mrs Wainwright was a popular, although strict President of that useful institute.) "We kept it going until rather late I'm afraid, and what with all the clearing up afterwards, I didn't get back until after 11.00. He wouldn't have rung up as late as that, and besides ....." Inspector Morris awaited some great revelation. "The Colonel did like a drink or two when he stayed at his club, especially if Brigadier Horner was there!"

Inspector Morris glanced at his notebook. It didn't seem to have much in it. "Did the Colonel have any, er, enemies. People who had a grudge against him. Anything of that sort?"

"I wouldn't have thought so. When he was in the army he had the reputation of being a very easy-going officer. When he was a Company Commander, I remember his Colonel telling him that he should be harder on defaulters. My father, the General, thought that Maurice was — well, rather soft. But he was very strict about dishonesty and corruption and all that. Very strict.

Of course, he had a terrible row with the vicar here: not the present one. The one before."

"What was that about?"

"Bells. The vicar wanted to ring little bells during the Holy Communion, the Sanctus, you know. Well, Maurice hated all that sort of thing. 'Bells today, smells tomorrow,' he said. Meaning incense of course. He was, well, rather Protestant — Northern Ireland you know."

Inspector Morris did know. Before he joined the police force, he had served as an Infantry Corporal himself and had done a tour in Belfast. He closed his notebook. A thought occurred. "We'd like to go through his papers. One of my officers will call this afternoon. By the way, did the Colonel take the letter from the stockbroker with him?"

"I don't really know. I never saw it close-up. He was very careful about letters and would put the day's mail in that pigeonhole." She indicated a battered desk in the corner of the room. "Then he would file them away if they were important." The pigeonhole was empty.

"We didn't find any letters when we.... when we examined your husband's body. We had better see his stockbrokers. They may have been the last people to have spoken to him."

"Laurence and Latham, Fetterlane, I think. He'd been with them for several years."

Inspector Morris took his leave still marvelling at the calm demeanour of the Colonel's widow. His own wife was a woman of powerful emotions which she expressed loudly and long. Sometimes it could be tough but the Inspector liked to think that if he were found murdered sorrow would be visible. Could she know anything, he wondered? President of the WI? Ridiculous!

Two telephone calls by the police produced surprising results. The stockbroker had not written to Colonel Wainwright. No, not for some time. They were distressed to read of his death in the newspaper. A most valued client. The Regular Army Club's secretary was equally clear. The colonel had not been in the club for some months. A fine officer and gentleman. Will be much missed. Would the Superintendent let them know the date of the funeral? The members always sent a representative and a wreath.

Bridgeminster railway station could give no help. The booking office clerk on duty on the morning of the murder thought he might have sold a ticket to someone like the Colonel. The ticket collector on duty in the afternoon remembered nothing.

No, he never noticed passengers, except on Saturday when he had a list of dangerous football fans to look out for.

Sir Richard Smith heard of the murder at 5 pm on the day of the discovery. Mrs Sellers knocked on the door clutching a crumpled evening paper. He had just returned to the flat after another troublesome interview with his bank manager who had besought him, with genuine tears in his eyes, it seemed, to do something about investing the vast sums accumulating in his bank account. He reflected that he really must get rid of some more of it. Another cheque to Father Randall? It was difficult. He had also called at the travel agents. He had heard of Activity Holidays — "Golfing in Scotland". He had always thought a golf ball to be a ridiculous little missile. "Learn to fly in the USA" — that sounded rather dangerous, as did "Beginning Mountaineering in Austria." Still, he would have to do something. He was studying the glossy brochures when Mrs Sellers called. She was very excited.

"Have you heard, Sir Richard? My husband knew him! He was on the Bench when Edgar had his bit of trouble with the car. Ever so sympathetic and quite a small fine really. Who would want to kill him? In the Park: the Abbey Gardens of all places. I walked around there just before Christmas. Just think who could have been lurking in those bushes!" She rattled on as Richard tried to read the front-page report. "I expect you'll want to see the scene of the crime. I'd be too scared to go near the place. You'll soon have a theory about the murder, I'm sure. I told Mrs Lummus about you finding the thief who took my things and she said she never believed policemen had much sense anyway! Her husband was a policeman!"

When his neighbour had gone, Richard sat in his armchair before his electric fire. He poured himself a modest glass of sherry — real sherry now rather than South African, although he still couldn't bring himself to pay more than £4.50 a bottle. He re-read the report of the murder which Mrs Sellers had left with him. He knew Colonel Wainwright, or at least had met him, for the Colonel had for a time, been a governor of Alderman Grimshaw

Comprehensive. He had resigned angrily when Mr Bender, the new headmaster, had refused to make any mention of Armistice Day at the school assembly. It really was a fascinating crime, Richard reflected. Not quite an Agatha Christie setting nor really one from Dorothy Sayers. One for Mr Campion perhaps? He would certainly walk round the park tomorrow. He rose from his chair and entered the kitchen. It was too cold a night to walk down the road to the Kai Lung Chinese Takeaway or the Star of India restaurant. He selected a packet of frozen Chili Con Carne from his deep freeze and opened his microwave.

Chapter 5

Next day the three detectives met. "No motive, no evidence, no nothing," said Superintendent Garrett gloomily.

"He's talking about bringing in The Regional Crime Squad." He was the Chief Constable, Sir Gregory Ogmore, recently knighted for having served on a number of government commissions of enquiry and being notable for having, by his tedious obstruction, prolonged their work by several years.

"We don't know who sent that letter, if there was a letter. His wife didn't see it. We don't know if he got to London or whether he really went at all! Nobody remembered him at the railway. If he'd looked like a proper Colonel, moustache and all that, it would have helped." In fact, Colonel Wainwright had not been a typical military man in appearance — five foot seven inches, balding, spectacles, dark suit — he was very ordinary. "And if he had a letter, where did it go?" asked Morris; he wouldn't have thrown a business letter away, if it was a business letter. Perhaps it was from a woman and he told his wife ....?

"He was seventy one remember," put in Polk.

"Doesn't mean a thing," pronounced the Super. "Remember that case we had; when was it, seven or eight years ago? He was eighty plus!"

They remembered. It was one of their more enjoyable affairs.

"And how did he get into the park? It was shut at 4 pm. He died around midday, or that's what the doctor says. If he'd been alive he would have frozen to death that night. No need to kill him. If he was put in there dead, how did they get his body over the wall? Spikes everywhere. Get the canteen to send up some tea, Jim." Polk knew his place and went off to get some refreshment.

Polk spent the rest of the day examining every inch of the railings around the Abbey Park. It was not enjoyable particularly as the snow had gone. A thin rain fell steadily. He also had another chat with the park-keeper. Harry Marder claimed that he had locked the park gates as usual at about 4 pm.

"Well a bit earlier perhaps. No one in the park on that sort of day."

"Who had keys?"

"Only my set and the ones at the office." He showed the detective a massive key to the great wrought iron gates installed in 1893.

"Where do you keep the key?"

"On the hook by the back door."

"Were you at home all the evening?"

"Watching TV," said the park attendant, "and the back door was bolted. Always is."

Back at the station, he typed out his report and left for home an hour later than his usual time. He lived in a semi-detached house in the suburbs. His wife was not pleased.

"Your dinner's spoiled. Your mother rang four times and that tap you mended is dripping again. The Barclaycard account has come. I suppose you're going out again? How you expect me to keep cheerful when I'm alone most of the week I don't know ..... etc etc."

Laura Polk did not share her husband's love of amateur dramatics. 'Silly play-acting' she called it and Wednesday was always rehearsal night. Keen as he was, the Sergeant was not looking forward to a long rehearsal in the chilly Coronation Hall after his hours in the park. 'The show must go on,' however, and after his meal, (which was indeed ruined), he got out his car leaving his wife in front of the television.

There were two weeks to go before opening night. There was a lot of influenza about and the understudies were looking distinctly hopeful. Richard arrived early as usual, and took his seat in the prompt corner. Several of the more impressionable ladies in the cast loved being prompted by a real-life baronet, even if he was a former school teacher. Mary Lou McGregor, wife of the local GP and born in Connecticut, (how that dour Scot had found her was a great mystery), expressed the opinion that Richard was 'real cute'.

It was not a good rehearsal. Two of the cast had colds and could not make much of the northern accent required in that classic comedy. Willy Glossop does not have many lines but Arthur Polk had not mastered them. The cast was irritable and George Campbell, the Director, despairing.

There were no 'luvvies' and few 'darlings' that evening!

After the rehearsal, Richard met the detective at the door. "Come back for a drink Jim. I've got another bottle of that whisky you liked. The one with a bird on it."

"Ah, the Famous Grouse — what the aristocracy drink. I could really do with one. What a shambles this evening. George Campbell's losing his grip. You ought to take up directing — in your new position."

Richard's flat was two minutes walk from the Hall. Polk left his car and they walked rapidly through the damp streets.

"Help yourself. I'll get some ice for you." The Sergeant poured himself a treble and sank back into the new armchair.

"What a day it's been. Crawling around that bloody park all the afternoon, the wife's in a filthy temper and then the rehearsal! Not too much water, thanks." He sipped his whisky and Richard filled his small sherry glass. "We didn't find any funny matchsticks to help us, either! (Polk was never going to let Richard forget that matchstick.) Not a clue of any sort and no motive either, that I can think of. Who would want to do in a peaceful old boy like Wainwright?" Polk went on describing his morning's work in flagrant breach of the regulations covering confidentiality.

As the level in his glass sank, he gave Richard details of the investigation.

"He was on the Bench. Someone could have had a grudge against him," Richard suggested.

"Not against him! They say he was the softest magistrate in the district. Believed any tale. The local villains would have subscribed to a retirement gift when he stood down! Mind you, he was harder on motoring offences and especially strict on drink-driving."

Richard reflected that the Sergeant was well on the way to being over the limit himself but Arthur Polk was unworried. The Bridgeminster force had never had one of those unfortunate cases where a young constable with a breathalyser arrests a superior officer. It is called 'esprit de corps'.

"The thing is, we have to find out how it was done. How was that letter sent? How did he spend the day? How did he get into the park? If you know how it was done ......"

"When you know how, you know who!"

"That's very neat. You're own?"

"Not exactly, read it somewhere. Do have some more whisky."

"Thanks." The Sergeant poured reverently. Inspector Morris will have it that there's sex somewhere at the bottom of it, but I don't see it. When he was in the Met. he was in the Vice Squad, sees sex everywhere. Sex in the Abbey Park in the summer, yes — but, in January!"

"He might have had enemies elsewhere, from his army days or on the Council; and what about his sons? They stood to inherit a substantial sum."

About as likely as that you bumped off your uncle — the 'meat-pie king'. One son is serving in Germany and the other is — what do they call it — military attaché in Washington. The next thing that you'll suggest is that the wife did it! As to the District Council, I have been into that. Saw the Chief Clerk, Gutteridge, this morning. Calls himself, Chief Executive now. Crafty solicitor, but I got him to talk. They all hate each other on that Council, particularly those in their own party. They didn't love the Colonel especially but nothing really against him."

Richard took his second glass of sherry and considered. "Well, if you want a really sensational theory how about this? The Colonel had been in Military Intelligence. He once unmasked Igor Bumpofski, the great spy from Moscow. Now Igor is out of prison and intent on revenge."

"Ha ha, nice one. What you don't know is that we do always check when it's service personnel. Called MI something. The Colonel was plain infantry and not too brainy, Honest though and reliable. No more whisky thanks. I must get back to the missus. Must be nice and peaceful, the bachelor life. I can hardly remember it!"

Polk stood up quite steadily, to Richard's surprise.

"Thanks for the drink. See you at the next rehearsal. Go over that park thoroughly, for matchsticks!"

Polk left laughing heartily at his own joke.

Sir Richard Smith sat in front of his fire for the next hour. He picked up 'Death in No Trumps', a mystery novel by a new author. It was no good. By page forty he had satisfied himself that it was the man, supposedly from the electricity board, who had killed the Bridge-playing retired surgeon. He resisted the temptation to check his conclusion by looking at the last page. He put the book

down and thought about Polk's case. "When you know how ....."
But, in this case, there seemed no way of finding out the 'how'. Perhaps some new fact would emerge, but if not? He took down a writing pad from the shelf and scribbled a few notes. If you can't find out the 'how' surely it was right to concentrate on the 'why'? Had Polk considered all the possible motives for murder?

He made himself his nightly mug of Horlicks and went to bed.

Chapter 6

The psychologists can probably explain the reason, but it is an undoubted fact that if a man goes to bed wrestling with a problem, the answer will often come to him in the morning. Actually, it came to Richard at breakfast. Since his affluence, he had begun to make more of breakfast than in his teaching days. Then, it was usually cornflakes and toast. There were still the cornflakes and Tiptree marmalade now replaced the cheaper brand that used to be on his table. He now often added a cooked dish and that morning it was kippers and as he watched them cook, an idea came to him.

If that letter was what the deceased said then it was a forgery. Somebody must have known the name of the Colonel's stockbroker and been able to get a copy of their notepaper. As he ate his kippers he thought again about motives. Why did people kill? Leaving out 'crimes of passion', Richard was inclined to think that money was probably the root of all evil. But although the Colonel was moderately well-off, surely there was not enough wealth to tempt a killer? Now a fortune like that of his late Uncle Gregory might well tempt someone. It was not a nice thought.

After breakfast and hoping that the odour of kippers did not linger about his person, Richard called at his bank. The branch of the Royal Commercial was in the High Street, a dignified Georgian building, gutted and re-built internally in the bad taste shown by banks everywhere. The manager, an ageing yuppie named Ponting, greeted him warmly. "Sit down, Sir Richard, sit down." He flicked a switch on his desk which told his staff that he was not to be disturbed. "You've come about your account. I was looking at it yesterday. There is now, (here his voice dropped), about £60,000 on current account. "Is that bad?" Richard replied.

"Bad? No, not bad: that is, not bad for the bank. But we pay no interest on current accounts. You are losing a considerable sum — every day! Mr Ponting's grief was sincere. "But what do you suggest? I want to give a lot of it away but it keeps coming in."

"You could invest in the market. Share prices are depressed at the moment. It might be a good time to buy."

"I have been thinking about it for some time." (This was not strictly true but detectives have to use deception.) I shall have to have a stockbroker. Do you know any you could recommend?"

Mr Ponting named one or two well-known firms. "I will send you a list. Would you like to speak to our Investment Adviser? You will, of course, need a good firm of accountants. Your tax affairs alone, will be quite complicated."

Richard groaned. Until last summer, his tax return had only taken him one hour to complete. He had already had some baffling letters from the Inland Revenue. "Yes, you had better suggest a suitable firm. By the way, do you know a stockbroker called Lawrence and Latham?"

"Oh yes, in the City. Quite sound. A number of local people use them. We had a provincial stockbroker in Bridgeminster but he had to close down. A most unfortunate affair and Lawrence and Latham made arrangements to take over his clients. Have they been recommended to you?"

"Well, yes. In a way. Can you give me the name of a satisfied client?"

"Well I mustn't do that I'm afraid. Confidential business you see, but I can tell you that two or three of our local investment clubs use them."

"What is an investment club exactly?"

"Oh, a group of people get together, usually from the same firm. They pay a few pounds regularly into an account and the Club Committee selects a share each month. They have a lot of fun — not serious high finance. More of a hobby. Sometimes they show a nice profit. I was in one when I worked at Head Office."

The manager implied that he had now put away such childish things. "Your old school didn't have one, I believe. They have a very active club at Edward the Confessors." Now, St Edward's school was the other Bridgeminster comprehensive. It was in a better district than Alderman Grimshaw and was run by the Established Church. Middle-class parents were known to attend church quite frequently and even receive Holy Communion to get their children admitted. The headmaster always wore his gown and it was generally recognised that the school had a superior tone. The pupils wore expensive purple blazers and Richard knew one or two of the teachers.

That afternoon he rang the man he knew best. Martin Stuart was a rather exquisite young man who might have been the model for Carroll's 'Stunning Cantab'. At thirty years of age, he was already Head of the English Department and clearly destined for higher things. He was thoroughly Progressive in his views but always made sure he could not be accused of being trendy. He was married to a gorgeous and intelligent blonde named, Candida. St Edward's staff were usually married. The Bishop, a rather grim low churchman, frowned on 'stable relationships'. Since Candida was also Head of Social Sciences, their joint income, by teaching standards, was sensational. They had a Volvo and a sporty two-seater. Their flat was in the best, newly-developed block in the city and worth four times the price of Richard's.

Richard was beginning to think that he was getting quite good at deceptive excuses. "Martin Stuart, Richard Smith here. Long time since I've seen you. It must have been at that Teaching of English Conference, two years ago."

"Sir Richard! How nice to hear from you. What are you doing now? Given up the chalk-face I suppose? We heard all about your good fortune. Why don't you become one of our governors? The old man would love to have a title on the Board and you don't have to do much. In your new position ..."

"Well thanks, Martin, jolly kind of you to suggest it, but what I rang you about was this. I shan't be going back to teaching. I don't suppose they'd have me anyway, but you see, I have a number of texts — Shakespeare plays, Milton, Chaucer and so on — which I used to lend to pupils whose parents were not too well off. I thought you might like to have them."

"Oh, that's very kind of you. We don't do much with Milton and Chaucer here and of course, our parents are usually pretty generous. But I expect we can find a use for them."

"Good, I'll bring them round this evening if convenient. About 7.30 pm OK?"

"Fine, we'll have drinkies and you can tell us all your adventures. Wasn't there something about crime and matchsticks?"

"Forget that and you'll be doing me a favour! Just a sort of joke!"

"Ah, well. See you at 7.30 pm. Bye."

The flat was as beautiful as its mistress. Pale pastel shades, modern pine furniture and what looked like valuable modern paintings on the walls. There was a baby grand piano. Candida too was stunning in a long skirt and something shiny above. Her welcome was effusive although she only knew Richard by sight.

"Gin, Whisky, Vodka — there's Campari and — what was that stuff we brought back from Italy, darling?"

Richard murmured that perhaps they had sherry?

"Sherry?" said Candida doubtfully. There's some in the kitchen but I don't think ......"

"Oh, I'll have whisky then please. With water and not too much whisky. I've got to drive back!"

It went quite well on the whole. Martin said all the right things about the books. He had all the details of Richard's transformation, even to showing that he knew the amount of the new baronet's riches. Richard wondered how these things got out. "I suppose you have an awful lot of financial things to look after. It must be a dreadful bore for you."

Martin had no financial affairs other than a huge mortgage and the loan for the cars.

"Well yes, it is a worry. That was another reason for my coming to see you." He paused, amazed at his own cunning. "You see, my bank manager is bothering me to invest my — well, surplus income, and I heard that you had an Investment Club at St Edward's so I wondered if ....."

"It must be nice to have a surplus income," said Martin laughing. "Actually, I was in it until we got married then I had to sell out. Fifty pounds a month, I put in and just about broke even if I remember rightly."

"You've forgotten, darling, how clever you were when you were on the Committee. You told them to buy Eastern Oil and they just went up and up."

"Well, that was a lucky break but you wouldn't want to invest at £50 a month."

"No, but I thought you might be able to tell me about stockbrokers and so on."

"I kept a file with all the papers in it. I think I know where it is." He returned with a cardboard folder stuffed with papers. "Here you are. John Mitchell, the Deputy Head, ran the club you see and he got out this list every month showing the value of the club investments. Then we got one of these from the broker every month or so, with their suggestions."

He held up a letter with the printed heading, 'Lawrence and Latham, Stockbrokers'. "Look, why don't you keep the lot. It's two years since I dropped out and I was going to throw it all away anyway. Married men can't speculate!"

"You've got other expenses now, haven't you darling?" Her voice was deep and vibrant. Richard wondered about married life. She was an incredibly beautiful woman. He jerked his thoughts back to investments.

An hour later, with only one weak whisky inside him, Richard returned to his flat.

Chapter 7

The offices of Lawrence and Latham were not as impressive as those of Palgraves, Solicitors of Lincoln's Inn. Their welcome, however, was much more effusive. There was no Lawrence and no Latham, but the Senior Partner, Mr Goldman, had heard of the Smith millions! In fact, he heard of everything going on in financial circles. He welcomed Richard with a surprising choice of refreshments from a cupboard behind his desk. The sherry, Richard found to be inferior to Sainsbury's best. It is strange, thought the new baronet, how quickly one becomes accustomed to a life of luxury. Mr Goldman would be delighted to handle some of Richard's investments. He produced a number of handsomely printed prospectuses, asked for the name of Richard's bank and his accountants and then seemed disposed to chat.

"So, you live in Bridgeminster? A delightful old city. We have a number of clients there. How did you hear of us?"

Truth first, elaboration afterwards.

"Well, a friend of mine was a member of an investment club that did some business with you, and then of course, there was Colonel Wainwright."

"Did you know him? A very sad loss. A much valued client. Tragic, tragic." Richard hesitated. "Well, not personally you know but someone spoke of him as a client of yours."

Mr Goldman's voice dropped. "You may not know the details but I think I can tell you that our firm is involved, in a rather unfortunate way, in the Colonel's death." Richard feigned astonishment, with the satisfied feeling that he was getting better at deception with every opportunity.

"Indeed?"

"Yes," replied the stockbroker. "We have had the police here twice. Someone apparently sent Colonel Wainwright a letter purporting (and here he used that legal word solemnly) to be from this office and asking that poor man to come to see us, on the day of his death!"

"You had not written to him then?"

"No, certainly not. Somebody must have stolen a sheet of our notepaper because nobody here wrote to him."

"Did they show you the letter?"

"The police did not have it. His wife told them that he'd had a letter from us."

"Was the Colonel short-sighted?"

"Yes, I should think so. He wore thick glasses at any rate and he was rather deaf you know. He had one of those hearing aid things but he never seemed to get on with it. Always fiddling with the switch. He told me that he was blown up somewhere and damaged his hearing. We phoned him once about some government stock and couldn't seem to get any sense out of him."

There seemed no more to be discovered and Richard rose to leave. "I will be in touch, Mr Goldman, when I've talked it all over with my bank manager. For some reason he's very keen for me to invest my money." He moved to the door. "By the way, Mr Goldman, were there many investment clubs in Bridgeminster? Ones that you acted for?"

"Well, they seem to have gone out of fashion. Not so much money about now I suppose. One or two schools, Fergusons had one, (Fergusons was a large factory near Bridgeminster that made sweets), and of course, there's a very successful one at the Local Government Offices. The District Council, if I remember correctly, or was it County Hall? Come to think of it, it was Colonel Wainwright who put them on to us. They may be good at wasting public money but they made some pretty shrewd investments, I remember. They always seemed to sell out at the right time. Years ago, (and here he paused reverently), they sold Poseidon at the top. Clever chap ran it. Housing manager or something like that. Real risk taker. Pays sometimes."

Richard had never heard of Poseidon but he was prepared to join in the worship.

"Very impressive, Mr Goldman. I hope I can do as well when I invest with you."

The formalities were gone through and Richard feeling extravagant after this contact with high finance took a taxi to the station where he bought a copy of the 'Financial Times' and the 'Economist', to read on the train home. How boring money is, he concluded!

It was, though, while running through the columns of a newspaper, that a thought came to the would-be detective. The

Colonel had been a District Councillor and the District Council Staff Association had run an Investment Club. Someone in those offices would have had letters from Lawrence and Latham. It was a sort of link. Surely Polk and his colleagues would have thought of it? He must ask? And what did he himself know about District Councils. Did they get as angry with each other as did the Members of Parliament? Richard remembered the day he had taken '4 F' to visit Westminster, where they had behaved abominably. It had been a debate on the imposition of VAT on ice-cream. The pure hatred that the Front Benches displayed was amazing and as for the Back Benchers ....!

Were District Councillors like that? He must find out.

Chapter 8

The offices of the Bridgeminster Constituency Conservative Party occupy three rooms over a hairdressing salon in the High Street. The agent, a tall but drooping man of forty, was delighted to see Sir Richard. Sir Richard wished to become a member? Nothing easier. A form was filled in. The subscription? There was no specific sum — whatever Sir Richard thought suitable. A cheque was written and Mr Hambrook the agent, became even more affable. It is not every day that £500 is added to the constituency party's funds! "I hope you will be able to join in some of our activities. Apart from social events we have monthly discussion groups and Quarterly Political Education conferences. Last month we had a minister as speaker." The Minister had been the Under Secretary at the Ministry of Sanitation with special responsibility for polluted beaches but he had been a minister of sorts.

Richard gathered strength for a little more deception.

"You know, Mr Hambrook, I have always been a Conservative supporter except for a brief flirtation with the Liberals when I was fourteen, but now in my new position ......"

"Exactly, in your new position," murmured the agent. "I feel that I would like to take a more active part in, — er local politics. Maybe even standing for the council. Do you think I might have chance of a candidature in a marginal seat?"

They were all virtually marginal seats in the Bridgeminster District, since the rise of the Liberal Democrats, but Mr Hambrook felt that it would be discouraging to mention that.

"I am perfectly sure that we could find you a seat, either on the County Council or in the District Council. As a matter of fact, there are by-elections in both coming up."

"Oh, I think the County would be too grand for me. The District, definitely."

"Well of course, you will have heard of our sad loss. Colonel Wainwright's seat will be coming up in a month or so. I believe also, that Mr Partington-Brown is thinking of giving up. That would be for Bridgeminster South — quite convenient."

"Well, if you think I'm up to it?"

"Oh, our Selection Committee will jump at the chance of having you. I'll see the Chairman today. They meet this week. To tell you the truth there aren't many people in the Party who are interested in standing." There were actually none but Mr Hambrook too was an expert in deception.

"Do you think you could give me an introduction to some member of the Council? Someone with a lot of experience who would be willing to give me some background knowledge. I've never even attended a Council meeting! There is a public gallery isn't there?"

"Of course, of course. I'll get in touch with Mrs Oldrieve. She was Deputy Chairman and is now acting Chairperson since we lost the Colonel. A charming woman, you'll get on with her. Just let her talk and she'll tell you everything. There is a meeting of the full Council on Thursday at three o-clock."

If Sir Richard had previously surprised himself with his powers of deception, he now was appalled at his own bravery. In all his twenty nine years he had never made a speech in public. He had not even joined the Union at Oxford. Nor had he ever stood for Office. It was a dreadful prospect. But he need not let it get as far as that. Once he had found out about Colonel Wainwright's life on the Council, he could gracefully withdraw. Meanwhile, he must first see Mrs Oldrieve.

He did not have to wait long to meet that redoubtable lady. Two days later the phone rang and the Vice Chairman of the District Council began to talk. She was still talking forty five minutes later. Richard reflected that she must be very well off to afford her telephone bill. Her name she said, was Helen. Might she call him Richard, or was it Dick? (No one had ever called Richard, Dick.) She was delighted to hear that he was thinking of standing. She was sure that he would be elected. She then gave him intimate details of all the other Conservative Councillors, the unpleasant attitude of the Liberal Democrats and all about the sole Labour member.

She then went on to describe the achievements of the Conservative-controlled Council in establishing Leisure Centres, Homes for Unmarried Mothers, subsidised street-theatre performances and exchange visits to a delightful town in Southern France. Perhaps at last remembering her phone bill, she invited Richard to dinner with herself and her husband on the Tuesday of next week. Richard was rather surprised to hear of the husband. He seemed inappropriate.

It was not until she had hung up that the thought struck him. She had never mentioned Colonel Wainwright.

Chapter 9

Mrs Oldrieve was not, it transpired, a rich lady. She and her husband lived in a semi-detached house in the suburbs. It was as neat and tidy as you could expect of a housewife who spent most of her time in Committee meetings. The husband was totally insignificant although he had an impressive moustache. He was a retired engineer whose hobby was cooking. He had joined a Cordon Bleu course at the local College of Further Education and the Beef Bourgignon they ate was a result. Perhaps he had not quite grasped the instructor's explanation of the recipe but it was a pleasant enough meal. The husband did not talk. Mrs Oldrieve talked; about the District Council; it was her only topic of conversation.

"You see, Richard," she said. "Although we are all Conservatives there are, how shall I say, tensions from time to time. Just little tensions," she smiled apologetically. "We are all good friends really but we do have different interests." Her own interest at the present time was the development of a three-acre site in one of Bridgeminster's most select residential areas, as a hostel for battered wives. "I know some of them are a little difficult and there are just a few naughty children but I feel that people should be made to take a caring attitude to the problem and put up with just a small amount of inconvenience. Canon Bolding gave us such a moving description of the problem that most of us in the Planning Committee were quite persuaded of the need." Richard had heard of the Canon as an extreme left-wing cleric whose lack of faith in the articles of the Established Church was more than compensated for by his belief in Social Engineering. "But, I think we shall get it going — now."

There was a wealth of meaning in the word 'now' that gave Richard his cue. "Now?" he murmured. "Well, I don't deny that Colonel Wainwright was opposed to the whole plan. The Chairman of the Council sits on all the Committees and of course, he carries a good deal of weight. He was a difficult man to persuade." There was a glint in Mrs Oldrieve's eye that suggested a dislike of any opposition. "Did the Chairman oppose any other projects?" Mrs Oldrieve's reserve began to disappear.

"Oh, he was always against new expenditure. There is a certain type of Tory who takes a narrow view of everything. Now, I am in favour of economy and keeping down the rates and all that sort of thing, but things have to be done Richard: they have to be done."

Richard began to see that when Mrs Oldrieve wanted things to be done they generally were done. "So there were probably others on the Council who found the Colonel's attitude a problem?"

"Plenty," replied his hostess. "He could be a delightful man in many respects but he did not understand how things worked. And there was the question of entertainment."

"Entertainment?"

"Well, naturally the councillors are entitled to a little refreshment from time to time. We work very hard, as you will find out if you join us. Coffee and biscuits, the Colonel thought justifiable but he did not approve of wine and canapes or a free lunch when we went on visits. He would insist on paying for his share and it made people feel uncomfortable."

"So there were quite a few people who disliked him?"

Mrs Oldrieve's manner changed. Richard realised that he had gone too far.

"Oh, I see what you're getting at. How ridiculous! Of course, I remember. You're being a detective — I read about it in the papers. You caught a burglar didn't you? You remember, Geoffrey?"

Mr Oldrieve lifted his eyes from the plate of home-made icecream, imperfectly set, which he had been contemplating gloomily and nodded.

"You don't think anyone would kill someone simply because they do not agree with their arguments? Not even the Liberal Democrats would do that."

"You mustn't believe all that detective nonsense," Richard put in hastily. "It was really a sort of joke you know. One of my friends is a proper detective and he started it. I was just interested in the mysterious death. I read a lot of detective stories you know."

"So does Geoffrey, don't you dear?" Richard was able to switch the conversation to the subject of crime writers. Mr Oldrieve loved the stories of Simon Brett. Richard however, had always found it difficult to identify with the alcoholic actor-sleuth but they provided a topic whilst they drank their coffee. Mrs Oldrieve's mood he noticed, had changed. She became quite subdued and Richard felt she was no longer at ease. He wondered if she was more intelligent than she appeared to be?

Chapter 10

A week later, Richard sat in the public gallery of the Council Chamber. The meeting lasted a long time. The Chairpersons of the various committees reported on their work, most of which was passed without opposition. The sole Labour member was rather rude to the acting chairman but Mrs Oldrieve obviously knew how to deal with that sort of thing. Richard saw clearly that she indeed was more intelligent than she looked. In fact, she managed things rather well. But, it was exceedingly boring.

That evening, Arthur Polk dropped in. Richard had been hoping that the Sergeant would get in touch. He had laid in a bottle of extremely expensive whisky which was regularly advertised on the back page of the 'Telegraph'. Polk was impressed.

"The Macallan," he breathed reverently and poured about £2 worth into a tumbler. "If they ever give me promotion, I'll keep it in the house!" In fact, promotion was very much on Sergeant Polk's mind at the time. Superintendent Garrett would be retiring in a few months. It was generally assumed that Inspector Morris would take his place and then there might, just might, be a step up for Polk. "If only we had cleared up that Park business it would have done me a lot of good, being in on it from the start." The whisky always began its work quickly with Polk. "Do you know, this is the only crime that I've ever been in on, where there's not been one lead. Not a single thing to go on. I've worn myself out going over every bit of the ground. I have seen all the people involved two, three times. They are sick of the sight of me! Nobody liked the old boy — we know that, except perhaps his wife, and I'm not so sure of her. But nobody had a motive for doing him in."

"What about people on the Council?" Polk looked hard at Richard across the top of his almost empty glass. After a long pause, illumination came. "I get it. I thought it was funny when I heard you were standing for the Council. More playing at detectives — the great amateur shows up the force! Me, what was his name, Lestrade looking silly again? Now, why don't you join the Specials? Get a nice uniform and you could go round the pubs with one of our constables on Saturday nights bringing in the drunks — real police work!"

Richard poured him another ration of the priceless golden fluid. It helped, for the detective became even more confidential. "You don't think that we didn't ask about that? I've got notebooks full of what they told me. Of course, they didn't like him much but not so they would kill him. He was always obstructing their little pet schemes — calling for economy and protecting the ratepayers. One or two of the ladies were particularly bitter against him. Seems he clobbered their idea of a new Home for Unmarried Mothers. God knows, we've got enough of those in Bridgeminster," he said with feeling.

"And that letter. Who sent it? They must have been daft to try that trick. Ten to one he would have rung up his stockbroker and asked them what it was all about."

"Oh no he wouldn't," said Richard.

"Why not?"

"Because he was deaf."

"That we know. There was a hearing aid thing in his pocket."

"But he found it difficult to use. He also disliked using the telephone. His stockbroker never phoned him."

"How do you know that? Been snooping around their office? The Super won't like amateurs sniffing around his case."

"They happen to be my stockbrokers as well. Naturally, they take an interest. Just passing the time of day with them, that's all."

"That's all my eye! I know you." Polk passed his glass over for a refill. "Glorious stuff this." Richard was generous. There might be more to be learned. Polk however, had no new information. He went over all the facts, sadly. "Of course, if there was a letter from the stockbroker and we've no real evidence that there was, it must have been sent by someone who knew that he wouldn't check up by 'phone. Furthermore, they must have put something in the letter which would be sure to bring him up to London. "'Your chance to make a million', perhaps. I got an offer in the post like that last week. Clever swindle. You don't think it could be sex after all? The Inspector reckons that the letter was all a blind and that he was off to see a girlfriend somewhere and that the husband bashed him."

"What — at seventy two!"

"If you were a proper detective you wouldn't ask that. We've got a list of local dirty old men as long as your arm. Why, I could tell you ......" But Sergeant Polk had not had quite enough whisky to name names. "Just get it out of your head that it was someone on the Council who clobbered him. It's all a game with them. A sort of hobby. They don't get more than ten quid for each meeting. Most of them are retired people. Not a spot of 'malice aforethought' anywhere."

Richard had to admit that it was probably true but, somewhere there had to be malice.

Chapter 11

Bridgeminster Public Library, a dismal Victorian edifice, presented to the city in 1875 by the second Earl of Clapton, kept a full set of the minutes of the District Council. It was easy to explain to the librarian that as he was thinking of standing for election, he would like to make a detailed study of them. The Reading Room was full of students from the local college, busy copying extracts from books of reference into what they usually called their Special Projects. Sometimes they even referred to them as 'theses.' The librarian with the deference to rank that is still occasionally found in Southern England, provided Sir Richard with a table to himself in the quietest corner and for the next five days, he perused the files laid before him. Colonel Wainwright had been a Councillor for six years and Chairman for two. It was the minutes for the last two years that Richard concentrated on.

It was a grim task. The Colonel had indeed thrown his weight against any sort of new expenditure. Two years ago there had been the West Vale sewerage extension scheme. Seventy four houses in that area relied on cesspools and it had been proposed to extend the main drains in that direction. Colonel Wainwright had pointed out that cesspools had been considered adequate for many years, that no nuisance had been alleged and that only thirty of the residents had requested the proposed facility. He went on to speak of his experiences in the digging of carefully sited latrine pits during his Army service.

Richard noted that Mrs Springfield, (Liberal Democrat), but also a supporter of the Green Party during the General Election, said that they were heading for an ecological disaster! Perhaps he ought to meet Mrs Springfield. People got very emotional about that sort of thing. He had seen them lying down in front of bulldozers when they were protesting about the new by-pass. But surely not murder?

Earlier there had been the matter of the hostel for discharged prisoners. Here, the late Colonel had had a good deal of support from residents in districts where the proposed establishment was to be built. The Colonel had carried the day. 'The Chairman argued that the money was better spent on projects benefiting respectable citizens. In his experience it did not help the offender to pamper him.' Here, the Colonel had been violently opposed by Mr Partridge, Chairman of the local branch of the League for the Rehabilitation of Offenders. He was quoted as saying that 'the chairman's attitude is that of one who has no sympathy for the underprivileged who provide the majority of offenders.' He expressed the opinion that it was a good thing that the Chairman was no longer a member of the Bench. The Colonel, "I resent that, Sir!"

Would love of the common criminal drive a man to murder? Richard plodded on through the seemingly endless pages.

Two days later he found a sensational row. Indeed, Richard remembered reading about it in the local paper. The great Fillingworth swimming pool dispute had convulsed the world of local politics. Fillingworth is a small town or rather, a large village, and a powerful pressure group among its citizens wanted a pool. A large pool was proposed and most of the money would have to come from the District Council's funds. The two Fillingworth councillors were Tories but their seats were marginal. They had a strong case but as usual Colonel Wainwright opposed them root and branch. He pointed out that Fillingworth had the highest rateable value in the District. The people living there enjoyed high average incomes. They could well afford to pay for their own swimming pool from their own resources. The Bridgeminster pool was already heavily subsidised. The Colonel calculated that every time a citizen dived into the pool it cost the ratepayer £4.50. The Colonel would be pleased to explain his calculations to anyone who was interested. He would like to point out that his party, and the party of the majority of his fellow councillors, was the party of 'private enterprise' and was therefore, opposed to 'featherbedding'.

Here, the Colonel seems to have made a mistake. Five of the councillors were farmers. They all hoped that the Colonel was not referring to the grants made to the agricultural industry which sustained the health of the rural economy and enabled farmers to keep up the good old traditions of the English countryside. The minute clerk had filled pages with this sort of rhetoric but one speech arrested Richard's attention. Mrs Susan Palmer had been a councillor for three years. She was a cripple and confined to a wheelchair after a car accident. She had also been the mother of an only son. She argued vehemently for the pool. 'What's £3 million compared with the life of one child. Every year, children are drowned on our beaches and in our rivers. Swimming pools save lives. Does the Colonel have no feelings for the lives of the innocent?' It was powerful stuff.

As Richard read the minutes, something stirred in his memory. What was it? A child that drowned — about a year ago, perhaps or even eighteen months. He left his table and asked the librarian for the files of the local paper. It would have been in the summer, June or July. He worked through the fading pages. It was there. 'Tragic Death in Brook'. It told of the death of ten year-old Graham Palmer found drowned in a deep pool of the small river that ran around the edge of Bridgeminster. He had built a raft with his friend. When the raft tipped, the friend had run for help but before it came the boy had drowned. A tragedy, — but- Richard pondered. Here was a motive for murder .... A sorrowing mother, her only child lost. Hatred for the man who had opposed the pool where children should learn to swim. A cripple too, who would have time to brood and be obsessional no doubt. But a cripple could not strike down an active man even though he was elderly?

A conspiracy then with other people involved, perhaps a husband? It sounded fantastical but where could one find a better motive?

One can do a lot of detecting in a good public library. There was a list of District Councillors with their addresses and telephone numbers. The electoral roll showed that there was a husband, one Ronald Victor Palmer MBE. The MBE made him sound respectable. Richard strolled round to the office of the conservative agent.

Mr Hambrook was unusually busy. There was talk of a possible General Election, one of his secretaries was about to take maternity leave, three by-elections for council seats were impending and the Branch Treasurer had just reported an alarming drop in subscriptions. The agent, remembering Richard's magnificent donation was however, willing to find time for the baronet-candidate. "Everything is going smoothly in Bridgeminster South," he assured his visitor. "The leaflets will be ready next week.

Weather's getting better for canvassing. I've seen the Chairman of the Branch today and he's quite optimistic."

This was a plain lie. The Chairman, a retired publican given to plain speech, had declared that he would take three to one against a Conservative getting in again. "There's a rough element in Bridgeminster South who won't vote for 'toffs'."

The 'toff' in question, was not particularly interested in the possible result, although he was not going to let the agent know that. "What I called about, Mr Hambrook, was to ask you if you could get me an introduction to one or two members of the other party. I suppose one should get to know something of the other side's point of view." Mr Hambrook stared. He had never heard such a point made. It sounded somewhat subversive. Still, there was that subscription. "Well, there are one or two who are — well — fairly reasonable, I suppose." He took from the drawer a list like the one Richard had found in the library. "Now, Petherbridge, he's quite sane. Old Mr Ambrose perhaps? No, you wouldn't get on with him. (The agent did not explain why.) There is one Labour member you know. Alf Potter, nice old boy but..... and there's Mrs Palmer, you'd like her — a very sad case that."

"Yes, I've heard her name mentioned. I think I've met her husband somewhere. Small man, slightly balding isn't he?"

"No, you've got the wrong person. Big chap. He was an Olympic something or other, twenty years ago. He won a gold medal for some event, or was it a silver, and got the MBE. He used to do a lot of athletic coaching but he's had to give most of it up to look after his wife. He's got a part time job at Fergusons and coaches their football team. There was a terrible car accident then they lost their only child. He was drowned."

Richard made sympathetic noises. "I think I'd like to meet the lady. Is she able to get about?"

"She's got one of those electric carriages. In fact you can see her about the town on most days. She helps in one of those charity shops in spite of her handicap. 'Paraplegics Aid' in Broad Street. You'll find her there two or three mornings a week." Richard left the agent and walked round to Broad Street. The charity shop was busy but there was no lady in a wheelchair.

The Abbey gardens were just around the corner and as it was a sunny February morning with just a hint of Spring, it seemed a good opportunity to take another look at the scene of the crime. The park is roughly circular and one of the City's quieter streets runs around two thirds of the circumference. Within the walls, a gravel path about ten feet wide, follows the railing on the inside. The railings of heavy cast iron, painted green with spikes and a thick-set hedge was planted inside them between the railings and the path. It would not be easy to climb over it, Richard reflected, much less to transport a body across. A body must have crossed over those railings on that Winter night unless ......unless they, (Richard was already thinking of 'they'), had a key to the park. What had Polk told him about the keys? One with the caretaker and one in the office? The District Council offices, of course. Always the District Council!

A little further on there was a gap in the hedge where a small hut stood against the railings. It was very small, about eight feet by five and six feet high. More of a cupboard than a hut, used no doubt to keep tools or a lawnmower. The door was padlocked. The roof was within a foot or so of the top of the railings. Anyone wanting to get over the wall from the inside could scramble to the top with little difficulty and then jump down. It would not have been easy to get in from the outside and not with a corpse to move, surely?

Richard looked carefully at the rough wooden planks of the hut. No significant marks, no bloodstains, no fragments of cloth caught on nails. A very plain hut. He looked behind the hut into the narrow gap between it and the hedge. There were a number of toffee wrappers and empty crisp packets blown there by the wind. The only other article was what appeared to be a piece of linoleum, triangular in shape and brown in colour, seemingly broken off a corner and about eight or nine square inches. It did not look promising but a clue is a clue. Richard put it into his pocket, slightly cheered. He walked home, buying muffins at 'Sally's Pantry' for tea and the piece of linoleum, neatly labelled, joined the bent matchstick in his bureau drawer.

Chapter 12

The Bridgeminster Theatre Club's production of 'Hobson's Choice' was not one of their greatest achievements. Arthur Polk never mastered the northern accent; sometimes he was pure cockney. The three ladies playing the Hobson daughters, hated each other as much off-stage as they were supposed to in their parts. As for Hobson himself, played by Emerson Cartwright, a retired estate agent, it can only be said that his attempt to model his performance on that of the late Charles Laughton, had only resulted in his being wildly, 'over the top'.

The usual party after the last night had been a glum affair and Richard persuaded the detective to leave early and come back for a drink. An even more expensive whisky did not at first cheer Polk. In fact, he criticised it severely. "Not nearly so good as that Macallan you gave me. Got to economise eh? Feeling the pinch — I know what it's like." His heavy humour failed to enliven him.

It took two stiff measures of Scotland's most famous export to relax Sergeant Polk. Apart from the disastrous production, he had other troubles. The promotion prospects were not looking too good. He feared that there were too many bright young men coming into the Force, 'graduates too!' "What good are degrees for police work? Book learning and theory. Now you've got degrees and all that. How would they give you a better chance of finding out what bent matchsticks might signify?" Polk was never going to let that joke be forgotten but it gave Richard the opportunity to bring the conversation round to the Park murder. It was time to put his theory.

"Well, it seems to me that the motive is the vital thing. If it wasn't money or sex, it could only be some sort of personal grievance and the obvious field for that is the dead man's work on the Council. I have heard that he aroused a lot of antagonism for his opposition to people's 'pet' schemes."

"He did, we know that. But you're not suggesting that half the councillors made a conspiracy to do him in? They wouldn't have the nerve, or the brains, most of them."

"No but what if there was one — say rather unbalanced person — nursing a grievance and becoming neurotic about it?"

"We thought of that and went through the list. I talked to Gutteridge for hours. He knows all their funny little ways. They say you're going to stand for the Council. Better you than me!" The Sergeant sipped thoughtfully. "Perhaps this whisky's not so bad after all!" he said as held out his glass, "and what's more this job was done by someone violent, probably big and powerful. They bashed his head in and got his body into that Park, somehow. Must have gone over the fence unless they'd managed to get a key. On a cold night too. Most of those councillors are pensioners. It really doesn't make sense."

"Could they have had a key?"

"Well there were only two. Harry Marder had one and he swears it was on the hook in the kitchen that night. The other was at the Council Offices in a glass-fronted case, in the Parks Department along with a lot of other keys. We checked that no-one had made a copy. No traces of wax or anything. It's not so easy to get a copy made of one of those big old keys. We asked all the locksmiths in the district."

"Was there anyone who could say that the office key was there on the day of the murder? Or the day after?"

"Of course we asked that too. What you detective story readers don't realise is that people never notice things like they do in books — you ask if anyone saw it on the hook in the morning of the 20th and all they can tell you is that they think it was there — they were all girls in that office anyway." Polk's attitude to the weaker sex was not exactly politically correct. "You can get used to this whisky after all," he added and Richard took the hint.

"Suppose, just suppose, that a Councillor was the killer. Could one of them get into the office and remove the key?"

"We asked that. Some of them are always wandering in and out bothering the clerks with their pet schemes. Gutteridge says that they get pretty smart about hiding when they see them coming. But don't forget whether that body got into the park through the gate or over the wall, it took at least two people to move him. He weighed over twelve stone even though he was short. You can't make me believe that any two of those people on the Council would co-operate — not in crime, anyway."

Marvelling at his visitor's ability to think clearly after a number of large whiskies, (to say nothing of the peculiar punch provided earlier at the Theatre Club party!), Richard saw his friend out. He did not go to bed immediately but sat before the fire thinking. His new gas fire with artificial coals and flickering flames, seemed to aid thought a little better than the old two-bar electric. It had seemed very extravagant but his central heating had been very erratic. As he prepared for bed he wondered if he ought to get a better flat or even a house. His penultimate thought before retiring was of the elegant rooms in the flat of Martin and Candida Stuart. His very last thought was that a fine house would need someone like Candida. Sir Richard Smith Bart was developing.

Chapter 13

The next day was a Friday. Market day in Bridgeminster is a Thursday and the shops are quieter on Friday. Richard walked to the town and looked into the charity shop in Broad Street. Two ladies were busy but there were no customers. An elderly woman was sorting garments in one corner. On the other side of the room a dark-haired neatly dressed lady sat in a wheel chair behind a low table, apparently putting cards into an index. She smiled a greeting.

"Mrs Palmer, I believe? I hope you don't mind me disturbing you at work. I'm Richard Smith and I was given your name as someone who could give me advice. I'm standing for the Council and I wanted to talk to someone on the opposition side. They said you are broadminded enough to talk to a die-hard Tory!"

"Of course. I've heard about you." Her voice was soft and friendly and more youthful than Richard had expected. She was at least forty five. "We're not all fanatics on our side you know. Are you going to stand for Colonel Wainwright's seat or Mr Partington Brown's?"

"Mr Partington Brown's. They seem to think I will stand a better chance there. The Colonel wasn't very popular, I understand."

"I couldn't stand the man," she replied. She stopped as if remembering something. "But what did you want to talk to me about?"

"Oh, just to chat about local government work and to learn something of the other points of view. I'm afraid I've have always been a 'true-blue' Tory but I hope I'm not too narrow-minded!"

"Some of your party needs enlightenment badly. I must try and help in your education but I can't get out much, as you can see. You must call on us one evening. We don't entertain since — since my handicap. Come round for coffee tomorrow evening. You know where we live?"

The Palmers' house was a bungalow, obviously arranged for the convenience of the disabled housewife. On the driveway stood a large station wagon with a high roof and a sort of lifting device to enable a wheelchair to be loaded. It was new. The garage door was open and a smaller car could be seen inside. The Palmers did not seem to be short of money.

Ronald Palmer greeted him. He was a very large man with powerful shoulders. Although in his forties, he looked an athlete. He confined himself to conventional pleasantries. In the sitting room there were several trophies in a cabinet and an Olympic Bronze Medal in a frame. A photo of a nine-year old boy was prominent above the mantelpiece, obviously the son they had lost so tragically. A ginger and white cat sat on the hearth rug. The Palmers too, favoured flickering gas fires. On a side table lay piles of papers which Richard recognised from his researches at the library as minutes of Council Meetings. "They keep coming every day," said his hostess apologetically. "If you do get on the Council you'll have to get a larger letter box! You're going to have a fight on your hands though. We've got Adrian South as our candidate. He fought a Parliamentary seat in Wales once and saved his deposit."

Richard acknowledged that achievement in the land of song and solid Labour majorities and admitted that his lack of experience was a great handicap. "You see, Mrs Palmer, I'm a Tory and always have been, but I'm not sure how Conservative principles should be applied to local affairs. What I really wanted to ask you or rather, have you tell me, is the real difference in attitude between the two main groups."

"I can tell you that in a nutshell," she replied. "You remember what that Thatcher woman once said? 'There's no such thing as society'? Well, that's the difference. I admit that not all Conservatives think like that, but enough of them do." Richard had as much reverence for the Blessed Margaret as for any politician but thought it better not to respond. He nodded gravely and she went on rapidly. "They oppose any spending of public money for the general good. Everything is reduced to commercial values; the welfare of the elderly, rehabilitation of offenders, birth control clinics, sports facilities for the young — all get opposed." Richard saw his opportunity. "I agree about the last. I was thinking of trying ice-skating but there isn't an ice-rink for forty miles!" Richard had no sense of balance and skating seemed to him boring but the story was unlikely to be challenged. "You campaigned very strongly for a swimming pool at Fillingham, I believe? I think I would have supported that."

"You would. Any decent caring person would have done but your late Chairman fought it to the end. But now he's gone." She paused, "We must try again." Suddenly, as she talked, the ginger cat jumped up and ran across the room to the door. Richard's eye followed it and his attention was caught by the image in a large mirror on the wall opposite. It showed Ronald Palmer's face which was turned towards the photograph of the child. For a brief moment that face showed — what? Anger, fear, sorrow? Richard could not say, but powerful emotion certainly. It was over in an instant but Susan Palmer had sensed it too. Her manner changed. "I must get you some coffee. Could you eat a sandwich — or cake perhaps, Mr Kipling's only, I'm afraid. I don't have time for cooking these days."

She wheeled herself expertly towards the kitchen and her husband rose from his chair to help. From the kitchen, Richard heard a murmured conversation. The cat returned to the hearth rug and was disposed to be friendly. Richard liked cats. It must be nice to be properly domestic and have a fireside — and here his imagination conjured up a picture of someone like Candida Jarvis in her long skirt and something shiny above it. The thought was instantly suppressed. Holmes would never have let himself be distracted like that!

The Palmers returned with a clatter of coffee cups and the three chatted. They asked about his life since he had left teaching. He told them about his world cruise. When he mentioned calling at various foreign ports it appeared that Ronald Palmer knew most of them. He had been a regular officer in the Marines, retiring in the rank of Major. His athletic triumphs had been won while serving as a young officer. "They give you lots of time off, you know: it's good for recruitment!" What was the particular branch of athletics? The Major had gone in for javelin throwing and the shot put. "But, I tried most of them. Even a bit of weight lifting."

The coffee was good and Richard much preferred the products of Mr Kipling to home-made cakes. His childhood memory of his mother's heavy sponge cake, (her only recipe), was vivid. The conversation dragged and Richard tried to find a way of bringing up the subject of investment — stocks, shares anything to do with finance. His hosts however, showed no interest. Neither would they resume the discussion of Local Government Affairs. They ended up talking about cats!

Chapter 14

Back at the flat, Richard sat with his Horlicks, considering. On a sheet of note paper he sketched the case against the Palmers. First, the motive. Psychology was something he knew little about. His favourite authors were from a time when the word was hardly known. Surely though there was something called obsessive hatred, triggered by grief or jealousy? The man had opposed the wife's scheme for a swimming pool; their child had died because it could not swim. They felt guilty and the guilt had been suppressed and turned into hate. It sounded plausible. Perhaps Father Randall would agree, with his experience as a confessor?

Secondly, the opportunity. Ronald Palmer had a part-time job with Fergusons. Fergusons had an Investment Club which used the services of Lawrence and Latham. He might have been a member and could have easily got hold of one of their letters. He was a powerful man and a trained athlete. He had, been a weight lifter. Not many men in Bridgeminster would be able to get a twelve stone corpse over the park walls: Palmer could. He had been a Marine, trained no doubt in unarmed combat. He would know where to 'strike to kill' with a single blow. Also, there was something intangible, but real. His face had shown something and the wife had seen it. Lastly, they owned a large estate car. Convenient for transporting a body.

He read through his notes and then tore the sheet into small pieces, putting them into the wastepaper basket. Richard did not know much about law but he had heard of libel. The damages could ruin a man. He went to bed. His last thought was that all the detective stories he had ever read ignored the real problem. How could anyone find out what a man was doing on a particular night, two months ago? Could he himself remember what he himself had been doing? Trying hard, he fell asleep.

For three days, Richard worried over his theory. Then he rang Polk and invited him round for a drink. The detective had not been so frequent a visitor recently. He had troubles to contend with. His wife had been dropped by DC Bosworth, as that ambitious detective, had his mind firmly fixed on the coming promotions. This fact made things more difficult for Polk. His own little affairs with ladies of the Theatre Club always went more smoothly when his wife was occupied elsewhere. Married life is all a matter of adjustment.

Superintendent Garrett too, was being difficult in his last months before taking up his pension. The Park Murder failure had soured him. He had wanted to go out with a bang. Polk had found himself being given the dullest cases to investigate. For the last ten days, he had dealt with three matters of Living off Immoral Earnings.

Richard made sure that that the supply of the Macallan was sufficient, before his visitor arrived, but the first glass or two did little to cheer Polk. To add to the Sergeant's troubles, the Theatre Club had decided to try their hand at Restoration Comedy. Polk knew his limitations and had not attended the auditions. "It's awful stuff — real filth I can tell you. In the old days the Porn Squad would have closed down any theatre putting it on." Richard sympathised. He had read Restoration Comedies enough at Oxford to persuade him that Bridgeminster Theatre Club could not cope with it. They would probably try 'Hamlet' next!

Deviously, Richard brought the conversation round to the subject of crime. They talked in a desultory way about a sensational killing in high life which the tabloid newspapers were featuring. A well-known TV personality, (and former government minister), had been interviewed by the police. Polk was scathing. That sort of case is no problem. The Met. should have cleared it up in half a day. All that crowd, TV, actresses, politicians, can't help talking; high on pot and cocaine most of the time. Now, here in Bridgeminster, they all clam up! I've interviewed thirty-five, no, forty people on that Park case and not one lead, not a single one." He regarded his almost empty glass gloomily. Richard saw his chance.

"You know, I've got a sort of theory about that, just an idea."

"You've not been going around looking for ……..?" Richard was not going to let him have that joke again. "No seriously it seems to me when there are no clues, you must look for motive. Now, we know that a lot of people disliked Colonel Wainwright but none of them were likely to have hated him so much as to want to kill him." Polk nodded agreement and looked so pointedly into his empty glass that Richard hastened to refill it. "Now," he went on, "if among those people who disliked him, there was one with — call it an obsession, unbalanced, brooding perhaps over some real or imagined hurt, someone intelligent, bold and very powerful. That might be the one to look for." Polk was mildly interested. "Have you got anyone in mind?" he asked. "You read that sort of thing in detective stories but you don't get it in real life. Sex or money, that's the usual."

Richard took the plunge. "Now look Jim," he said, "this is just an idea. I'm not accusing anyone. That's your job. The person I have in mind is well — a nice sort of chap, I think. Nice wife, too. It isn't even murder perhaps. 'Balance of mind disturbed, diminished responsibility' and all that, a very sad case." Carefully, Richard set out his case against Major Ronald Palmer.

Polk was mellow enough to give him some attention. He both knew Palmer and liked him. "He helped to coach our entry for the London Marathon. Great sportsman, always willing to help any sporting activity. Now if you'd said the wife, I could have understood that. Crippled like that, she might well be given to brood over things. The loss of the kid and all that. She couldn't have lugged a body about, that's certain. It just doesn't make sense."

"You wanted a motive. I agree that it's far-fetched but can you think of a better? And I swear there was some powerful emotion working in him. I saw the look on his face when his wife talked of swimming pools." Polk lay back in his chair and closed his eyes. He was not a quick thinker and was slow to grasp a point, but when he did get hold of something he stuck to it. After all, no one in the CID had put forward any theories. Only Inspector Morris persisted with his theory that sex was at the bottom of it. In all of his experience he had never known of such a motive that Richard was trying to establish. But, there might just be a chance. He opened his eyes. "Have you thought what a rumpus there would be if we took it up and we were wrong?" he asked. "They'd have my stripes off me and back on the beat." Polk could not think of anything worse than a return to the uniformed branch, but he also thought that if Richard was right then promotion was a 'cert'. Polk did not like decisions of that sort.

"I don't believe I've got the nerve to put it up to the Super. You don't know the scandals we've had when we've questioned the wrong suspect. There was that Mrs Parfitt —" he finished with a shudder. Polk had been a very young detective during that 'cause celebre' and had had to bear only a small part of the blame. All Bridgeminster had felt the deepest sympathy for that injured lady and cheered her successful action against the police for malicious prosecution, assault and battery, false imprisonment and several other wrongs which her expensive lawyers had plausibly argued. The damages had been sensational.

Richard saw the point. "Well, I suppose I've been too imaginative. Have another drink, Jim. How are they getting on with the new play?" Polk however, although he did not refuse the topping up, was in no mood to discuss the shambles which the rehearsals of 'The Country Wife' were producing. He was obviously brooding and he soon made his farewells. Richard went to bed wondering whether he had done the right thing. As he lay restless, he went over in his mind all the points he had made. It still looked a sound case.

The 'sound case' lasted for only three days. Even before his inheritance Richard Smith had always relaxed on a Saturday morning. Most teachers do and the habit lingers. He was drinking his second cup of instant coffee, (he had quite failed to produce a drinkable cup from the expensive machine he had bought), and was completing the 'Telegraph' Prize Crossword, when his doorbell rang. The ring sounded agitated. It was Polk.

"Well, you have dropped me in it," were his first words as he sank into a chair. The man was obviously very disturbed. "You mean — you did look into it. It wasn't him?"

"Wasn't him? It was never anything to do with him or the bloody swimming pool. Do you know where they were that day, and the day before, and the day after? At one of those Health Farm places where she goes for therapy for her legs. Three days they were there. Dozens of witnesses. He goes with her for company." Richard spooned coffee into a mug and poured hot water. The detective took it, and gazed into its depths gloomily. "They're all after me — from the Chief Constable downwards."

"You didn't arrest them?"

"Of course not. Just asked a few polite questions. They didn't like it though, naturally. We had to tell them what it was in connection with. She was the most upset. He's a real gentleman, not many of them left. He knows how to take that sort of thing. She won't forgive us though."

"You didn't," Richard began, "tell them about me?"

"No I didn't and I didn't tell the Super either. But you'll have to stop this playing amateur detective or you'll get into real trouble. There's a law of libel you know. We're alright if there are reasonable grounds for pulling someone in but you've got no protection."

To say that Richard Smith was shattered by Polk's news would be a grave understatement. It had looked such a fine theory. When the detective had gone, he sat and brooded. "Keep to matchsticks!" had been his last words, and the joke really hurt. It had all been a childish dream. Everyone knows there are no 'Lord Peters' in real life. Mr Campion, Hercule Poirot, Sir Henry Merivale are all, like the great sage of Baker Street, only fiction. When he went to bed that night, he looked with something like shame at the shelves of detective stories.

Chapter 15

The next day was Sunday. Sir Richard Smith stayed at home and continued to brood. The Sunday papers were filled with depressing articles and his usual Sunday crossword was too easy to amuse him. In the afternoon he even watched an old film on television. His troubles overwhelmed him.

How was he to get out of his commitment to stand for the Council? The election was only a few weeks ahead. Anyway what was he to do? What can a man with millions do? Father Randall had said that he could do anything. Politics bored him. Business would be absurd. The Law sounded dreary. Perhaps he should give it all away and return to teaching? That thought paralysed him. He became a very depressed young man. That evening he poured himself a glass of the expensive whisky that James Polk had so despised. He did not like the taste and it did not cheer him much. He remembered his mother warning him about solitary drinking, before he went to Oxford. Perhaps his father had been a solitary drinker? Why was he solitary?

Inevitably his mind conjured up the scene; a fireplace with a cat on the mat, two armchairs and a slim figure with fair hair dressed in a long skirt with something shiny above it, seated in the one opposite. It is to the baronet's credit that he never for one moment thought that his millions could supply that need.

Monday was always the day the dustmen called at Downview Court. The residents left their rubbish in plastic containers on the landings and the men emptied them into larger receptacles. They were a cheery crowd although they had to work much harder since 'privatisation', another reform demanded by the late Colonel Wainwright. Every Monday morning the clatter of emptying bins disturbed the peace of the flat dwellers. They often had a cheery word for Richard. Since his inheritance he had been a generous tipper; his last 'Christmas Box' had rejoiced their hearts. That morning he was finishing his breakfast, still feeling depressed. His mother's favourite aphorism had been, 'It will all seem different in the morning'. She had been quite wrong!

Suddenly, outside he heard a tremendous crash, followed by loud and prolonged curses. Leaping to his feet and rushing to open his door, he found a large and indignant dustman, clutching his wrist from which blood was already dripping. Mrs Sanders' plastic bag had burst and broken glass and other litter was scattered across the landing. The dustmen always wore heavy gloves but these had not protected the man's forearm. It was a nasty cut and the dustmen was giving his opinion about people who left glass bottles in inadequate plastic bags. He did not use many adjectives to describe such persons but the ones he did use were short and forceful. Mrs Sanders, a thin rather morose widow whose flat was on the other side of the landing, did not appear.

"You had better come in and let me put a bandage on that. It's Sam isn't it? It looks as though it might need stitches but we can stop it bleeding."

"Thanks Guv, that's very decent of you. What they call an 'industrial accident' — a week off on full pay I reckon." Richard led the man into his kitchen and reached for his first-aid box. Inexpertly he bandaged the wrist. "You won't be able to go back to work with that. I'll go down and tell your mates what's happened and ask them to clean up the mess. I'll get you a cup of coffee when I get back."

Sam had regained his usual cheerful nature by the time Richard had returned. He accepted a mug of strong coffee but rejected a drop of brandy in it. "Never touch the stuff squire. Too many of the lads waste half their pay down the Social Club and never have a penny saved. Now, I've bought my house off the Council and I've got a bit saved. By the time I take my pension, I'll have got rid of this mortgage thing and can take it easy." His great interest in life, it appeared, was pigeons. Richard rather liked him. "How's the job going now you're working for a private company?"

"Well, we've all got to work harder. To be fair I suppose, I'd have looked a bit closer at that sack in the old days. It's all such a rush now. Mind you, these new bosses don't worry so much about us doing a bit of 'totting'. The council office was always trying to stop it."

"What exactly is totting?"

"Well, you'd be surprised at what people throw away. There was that Arab who rented Kingsdown Lodge one year. He used to throw away a dozen soda-water syphons at a time. There's a couple of quid deposit on each of them. Well, we'd sort of 'rescue' them.

The council reckoned that they should have the value. Course, we always share out the proceeds, like we did with your 'Christmas Box'." Sam grinned in appreciation. "Some things people throw out can be real useful. I've got a carpet at home — genuine Persian my wife says. It only had a small hole burned in it and she did a lovely job with her needle. Looks fine now. Very good with her hands is Emma. Mind you she couldn't teach the girls, neither of them could sew a button on. Both schoolteachers now." Richard ignored this slur on his former profession. "Look," he said. "Your mates will have gone off with the lorry. I'll drive you home."

The offer seemed to upset the dustman. For the first time he used his host's title, "Oh no, Sir Richard, I'd mess up your car with these clothes on. I'll get the bus at the corner."

"Nonsense, I was just going out. It's only an old banger anyway. Where do you live?" It took several minutes to persuade Sam but eventually they got into the rather shabby Fiesta. Sam lived on the Marlbeck Estate, built by the Council in the Fifties but a fair number of the houses now the property of the former tenants, distinguished easily by the interesting additions made by the new freeholders. They talked about pigeons, the races Sam had won, their strange habits and the various diseases they suffered from.

Richard pulled up outside the house standing at the end of the terrace. The front garden was neat and the hedge well-clipped. Behind the house were the pigeon lofts. Sam's manner had changed. Now he seemed diffident and his vocabulary became almost refined. Perhaps, thought Richard, 'his Emma' was particular about that sort of thing. "Would you like to take a look at my pigeons Sir?" he asked. "I've got three real champions and some fine young ones coming on." They walked round the side of the little house to the gaily striped pigeon houses. The man was a real enthusiast. Richard heard not only about the races they had won but also about the races they ought to have won. He also heard about the unsportsmanlike attitude of the other fanciers. One house was empty. "I've just finished doing them up. This is the last one to get put right. I got this lovely bit of lino somebody dumped, — enough for all three houses and lots of bits left over. Real heavy stuff, not your ordinary house lino. Come from some office, I should think. Years of wear left in it. These business people are always throwing good stuff away. Messy birds pigeons. You need something thick under their perches: this is easy to keep clean."

They were indeed messy and Richard did not like the smell. Whatever he took up, he thought, it would not be pigeon racing! He thanked Sam for the interesting experience and made to leave, advising the dustman to get his arm seen to properly. Instead of driving home he turned towards the City and parked his car.

His gloomy thoughts were returning and he had a vague idea of calling at the Travel Agents. Then he remembered the election. Already six hundred and fifty households had received a blue-edged leaflet with his picture on the front page and a short statement on his views on local government written for him by Mr Hambrook, the Agent. He decided that he had better see Hambrook. How could he ask the man the best way to lose the election?!

Chapter 16

The Travel Agents were very keen to help. They pointed out that there was still some snow in the Alps. The holiday brochures showed both the delights of the snowy slopes and the apres-ski life. The pictures of the latter scene showed glamourous ladies, some of them blondes and in long skirts .... Richard was tempted but also considered a cruise among the Norwegian fjords and a safari in the Himalayas, led by an intrepid lady with thirty years' experience of Girl Guiding. He supposed that there would be no skirts, long or short in the mountains, but he took the brochure with a dozen others.

He lunched alone at the Angel Hotel, universally regarded as the best restaurant in Bridgeminster. The paté-maison seemed no better than that which he usually purchased at Waitrose and the sauce which garnished his Steak Chasseur was definitely inferior to the brand that Sainsburys supplied in the little jars which he used in his home cooking. Still, the ice-cream was excellent and the coffee better than his instant powder gave him. As he was finishing his meal, a man also lunching alone, got up from his table in the far corner of the room and made for the door. He stopped at Richard's table.

"Excuse me interrupting your lunch. You're Sir Richard Smith, I believe? I'm Neville Gutteridge, Chief Executive to the District Council. I've been wanting to meet you for some time. You'll be standing at the by-election in Bridgeminster, South, I hear?"

Richard stood and shook the lawyer's hand. It was a limp handshake but the man seemed friendly.

"I was just finishing my coffee. Could you drink another?"

Gutteridge took a seat, and a sign to the waiter brought another cup. The waiters at the Angel were very attentive to Sir Richard's needs. They appreciated his tips!

It was a rather strange conversation. They chatted about local affairs but Richard got the impression that there was something on his visitor's mind that he wanted to bring up. Gutteridge was in his forties, somewhat overweight, 'podgy', was the word that came to Richard's mind. He was neatly dressed with a rather surprising bow-tie, neatly manicured hands and slightly tinted glasses.

"Of course, I mustn't take sides but I was rather surprised to learn that you didn't stand for the late Colonel's seat. They are more true-blue up in Hangleton. Bridgeminster South is rather, more, — er — volatile."

"Oh, I don't suppose I stand an earthly chance of winning a seat anywhere. I'm getting cold feet now that the election day is getting so near!"

Richard had the impression that behind those dark glasses the lawyer's eyes were watching him carefully.

"Oh, I'm sure you'll do very well. I think you know some members of the Council already? Mrs Palmer was saying the other day that she had met you." Richard wondered whether the Chief Executive had got to know of the Police visit to the Palmers. The thought almost made him panic. He was learning how things leaked out — Palgraves, the solicitors; the unknown policeman who had told the local paper about the 'Case of the Bent Matchsticks'. Could this rather oily solicitor, have heard that he had put Polk onto the Palmers? Polk had said that he had told no-one. Perhaps Polk talked in his sleep?! If Gutteridge knew, there was nothing to lose. Richard took the plunge. "Who will be the new Chairman?" he asked.

"Well, I mustn't anticipate, but I think we may possibly get a lady Chairman, or Chairperson I suppose I should say. That really will be a revolutionary step for Bridgeminster."

"I suppose so. I have heard that the late Chairman antagonised many of the members?"

Again, Gutteridge looked thoughtful and paused before replying.

"Yes he did, I'm afraid. He didn't have the usual military mannerisms, but I suppose he was used to command. You can't run Local Government like an Infantry regiment."

Richard reflected that the Lawyer did not look as if he knew anything about soldiering. "My officers got on quite well with him, generally, that is. He was a most courteous man: you know. Old-fashioned courtesy. It's getting rarer every year."

Richard had not realised that Local Government clerks were called 'officers'. Of course Sanitary Inspectors were now Environmental Health Officers! Teachers would soon be

Education Consultants or something of the sort. As he drained his coffee cup a thought came. Was there one word emphasised in Gutteridge's last sentence? The smallest emphasis? "You said 'generally'."

"Well yes, there were some small difficulties. Matters of policy. Administration is such a complex matter today that the — er, amateur has difficulty in grasping the whole picture. Do you know much about computers?"

Richard knew nothing of computers. Secretly he felt that a gentlemen should not know anything about such things. His former headmaster had worshipped them and the result of computerising the school timetables had been two terms of near chaos.

"No, I'm afraid not. I'm not 'numerate' as they say. Scraped through 'O' Level Maths and left it at that." They chatted idly for a few minutes more, Richard getting the impression that Gutteridge had said what he came to say and was anxious to leave. "I must get back to the office. We're under great pressure these days! All this new legislation. It's been a great pleasure to meet you Sir Richard. I mustn't wish you all the best in the election — impartial you know! I can tell you that we always need well-informed members with time to spare. Goodbye."

The restaurant was emptying but Richard sat on thoughtfully. The hopeful waiters did not disturb him. A thought had come to him that opened up a new line of enquiry. He must look into it.

There were two ways to return from the hotel to the car park. Richard took the longer which passed the walls and fences of the Abbey Gardens. The flint-walled section hid the view of the neat flower beds now bright with spring flowers. Further on walls gave way to the heavy-spiked railings through which the passer-by could see the gravel path on which the body of the Colonel had been found. Here the pavement was wide and against the fence stood a green metal receptacle labelled 'Bottle Bank'. It was about five feet high with apertures labelled 'White', 'Green' and 'Brown'. On the other side of the fence was the small toolshed. The thing stood on four cast-iron wheels and it bore a poster with the District Council's logo, calling on the people of Bridgeminster to help in the great work of Conservation.

The people of the City had been helping. The section labelled 'Green' was full and smashed bottles lay around. Other things had been dumped near the containers; a broken pushchair, a number of damp cardboard boxes, a doorknob and a bundle of rags. Not a pleasant sight. As he stood looking at the mess a figure approached that he recognised as Henry Marder, the park keeper. Richard had spoken to Marder soon after the murder, had, in fact, bought him several pints in the Abbey Tavern and had been given a highly decorated account of the finding of the body. He remembered Sir Richard.

"Morning Sir."

"Morning Mr Marder." Not having the true upper class manner, Richard tended to 'Mr' everybody. "The park's looking very well. Lovely those daffodils. Pity about this nasty mess right by the railings."

"They're only supposed to bring bottles but they dump all sorts of rubbish here. Can't stop them. And boys. It was boys who tipped the whole thing over last month. No discipline — and the police don't want to know."

"How long has this thing been here?"

"A year, may be eighteen months."

"But surely it wasn't here last January? I remember after that horrible murder. I walked all the way around the park the day after."

"Ah, but it was Sir. That would be about the time it got broke and they took it away to be mended. Those boys again. One wheel broke right off. They've got a lifting thing that puts it on a truck. They had a new one there two or three days later."

"What date was that?"

"Couldn't say Sir. They always come to empty it on Tuesdays. It got broken after Christmas, about the end of January or thereabouts."

The park keeper suitably tipped, ambled away to his duties and Richard stood for a few more moments regarding the mess. Doormats, floor coverings, linoleum — linoleum! He took out his pocket diary. The murder had been on the 20 January. He had taken his investigative walk on the 22nd. The 22nd had been a Wednesday. He turned on his heel and almost ran to the car park.

Chapter 17

Back at the flat he opened his bureau and took out the envelope containing the piece of linoleum. He had found it between the hut and the railings. The bottle bank must have stood nearby. He had noticed it when he found the lino, but of course it was on wheels and could be moved.

As he turned the object over in his hands he remembered. Surely he had recently seen some floor covering of the same colour? Thick, dark brown, what they call 'heavy duty' — the dustman Sam and his pigeons! He had said that he'd found the lino somewhere, no doubt in the course of his duties. A whole roll of heavy lino. For a second time that day, a new thought entered his head.

That evening Richard parked his Fiesta outside the former council-owned home, on the Marlbeck estate. The door was opened by a motherly figure in her late fifties. "I am so sorry but I don't know your surname but I know Sam you see. I brought him home the other day after he had the accident. Just thought I'd call by to see if he's recovered."

The housewife's face was welcoming. "Oh, it's Sir Richard." She emphasised the 'Sir'. "It's Absey, but call me Emma. I'll go and fetch Sam. He's with the birds, as usual!" The little house was beautifully kept and furnished in remarkably good taste. Richard knew little about the private life of the working class. His mother had kept herself to herself and had discouraged "common" friends. He had expected to see ducks up the wall but instead there were reproductions of impressionist paintings and pretty curtains. There was a bookcase with paperbacks and solid-looking works on pigeon care. Mrs Absey returned. "Sam's gone to wash his hands. Those birds are so dirty. Would you like a cup of tea, or coffee I expect?"

"Tea would be marvellous."

"I've only got Lyons. Is that alright Sir Richard?" Richard was used to this. Since his title everyone expected him to demand exotic Chinese teas. He hated the stuff. "Lyons for me every time and please don't call me Sir Richard. Just Richard, Emma." Mrs Absey looked dubious. "You used to teach at Alderman Grimshaw's didn't you? You taught my Helena, that's our youngest. She's a teacher now." She pointed to a framed coloured print showing a pretty fair-haired girl in the gown and gaudy hood of a Bachelor of Education.

"I remember Helena. I only taught her for two terms before she left for college. Where is she teaching? She was a very bright girl."

"She's in a Comprehensive in Portborough. The children are a bit rough, she says, but you can't be too particular these days. Lots of her friends at college haven't found work at all. Her friend Teresa's working in a supermarket. Richard agreed that times were hard but privately told himself that a job in a supermarket would suit him better than a Comprehensive in Portborough. That city certainly had a reputation."

Mrs Absey bustled off to get the tea and few moments later her husband came in. His forearm was still bandaged. He welcomed Richard gravely and thanked him for the help on the day of his accident. His arm was better: he would be returning to work on the following Monday. Richard asked after the pigeons. The dustman was very ready to talk about his recent successes. Mrs Absey brought in the tea and biscuits, withdrawing discreetly to 'do the ironing in the kitchen'.

"Look Sam, I had another reason for calling on you but it's a very, well -er,- delicate matter. I would like to ask you some questions about your job but I wouldn't like the thing talked about."

"I heard you were going on the Council. If it's about the bits of fiddling the lads do now and again, I wouldn't want to shop them. It isn't much they get away with. I know it's against the law but nobody suffers and we don't get the overtime we used to."

"It's nothing like that Sam, but it is serious — very serious. You remember the murder in the park; Colonel Wainwright?"

"I wouldn't know anything about that. None of us had any love for him mind. He was the one who wanted the privatisation. Double the work and no more pay."

Richard put much sympathy into his voice. "I know, Sam and your chaps work hard. No one would think that you or your mates had anything to do with it. It's just that I've, —" he paused, "— worked out a sort of idea about the murder. I have a friend in the local police and we got talking. You remember you showed me your splendid pigeons? You said that you found some linoleum; heavy stuff, that someone had thrown out. Where did you find it?"

The dustman was still suspicious. "Nobody would have wanted it and it was thrown out where no-one's supposed to dump rubbish: except bottles that is."

"Look Sam, the lino's worth nothing. Nobody will bother about it. The point is I found a bit of lino like it which might be a sort of clue."

Sam seemed reassured. "Now where did I get that roll? It was a whole roll and good stuff. You wouldn't believe people would throw it away with years of wear left in it. It's a 'throw-away' society as any dustman will tell you."

"Can you remember where you found it?"

"Yes, I remember now. You remember that bottle bank thing by the park?" He stopped and stared at Richard, "By the park where the murder was."

"How was it lying?"

"In front of the container. There's a notice telling you not to leave anything except bottles but no-one pays attention. They leave cardboard boxes, old clothes, anything. No tidiness today, litter everywhere."

"What did it look like?"

"Well it was all rolled up neatly enough with a bit of string; no something like clothes line tied round it. I asked the lads if anyone wanted it but no-one did so I tied it on the lorry and took it home."

"Can you remember what day it was?"

"Well it was after Christmas. Towards the end of January. Cold it was, that day. I remember a touch of snow. It would have been a Tuesday. Tuesday's we clean up round that bottle bank and then the truck comes with the lifter and takes it away." Richard took out his diary. The body had been found on the 21st January. "Did you know there had been a murder when you stopped?"

"Not then. There were a couple of police cars parked in the road but we didn't think it anything special. We talked about the murder next day I remember. Richard took the envelope containing the piece of lino from his breast pocket. "I've got a piece of lino here Sam that I think came off that roll. You told me when you showed me your pigeons that you still had some bits that you hadn't used. Could you get me a bit?"

Sam was now looking worried; the look of one who is scared of getting too involved. He was a law-abiding man who had brought his children up to be honest and respectable but he had the instinctive distrust of the police that was typical of his social class. "I'll go and get a piece. I only kept the bigger bits. They're in the shed." He left the room and returned carrying a piece of brown lino about a yard square. Richard opened his envelope. It was the same lino. Sam was, by now, really frightened. "I won't get into any trouble about this will I Sir Richard? I've only got four years to go to my pension and nothing against me till now."

"No Sam, honestly, no one will blame you, but keep all the rest of that lino. You may have to bear witness that it's the same as the one in this envelope." Richard stood up. "I must thank Mrs Absey for a good strong cup of tea." That lady came in. She had obviously heard something of the conversation for she too looked worried. Richard made his goodbyes and prepared to depart.

He had just taken two paces down the path to the gate when the dustman called him back. "Look Sir Richard, I've just remembered something. We had some more rolls of that lino we picked up somewhere. Can't remember where but it was after the bit I had, I'm sure. It wasn't by a bottle bank or anything like that. Nobody in the gang wanted them so they went to the tip."

"Can't you remember where they were put out?"

"You know how many places we pick up from? Hundreds. Might have been some sort of shop or office, office probably. I'll ask the lads tomorrow."

"Careful what you say though. Don't say anything about the murder. I could be wrong and I don't want to look a fool and look, Sam, can I offer you something for your trouble?"

"No need of that, Sir."

"I know, but get something nice for Mrs Absey. Her home-made biscuits are great."

Reluctantly, Sam took the notes. It was only later when he counted them that Sam began to feel really troubled. Mrs Absey was about to have a real treat!

Chapter 18

The next day Richard sat long over his breakfast. For the first time he had an idea as to how the crime was committed. He had thought too much of motive when he had suspected the Palmers. After all it was true, 'when you know how you know who'. He was beginning to see the 'how'.

There were gaps though. What had happened to Colonel Wainwright between the time his wife had dropped him at the station and his death later that day? He was to catch the 11.10 am Polk had said. Did he catch it? Did he get to London? Was he killed in London and his body brought back? Unlikely. And who sent the forged letter that had lured him to his death? Who might have known that Lawrence & Latham' were the dead man's brokers? Richard felt the need of someone to discuss the case with. All the detectives in fiction had someone — Hastings & Watson, Bunter and Magersfontein Lugg.

Richard had not greatly admired the Perry Mason books but how nice to have a Della Street. He really must not let his imagination run riot! He ought to talk to Polk about his ideas but the Sergeant had been so scathing about the Palmers. It was a fine morning and Richard went out.

There are three shops in Bridgeminster which specialise in floor coverings. The largest is Moffats and Richard called there first. The youthful salesman looked as if he were deeply insulted at the proposal that he should sell anything. No, he had never seen anything like that bit of lino. It wasn't possible to match anything like that old stuff. Richard asked to see the manager.

The manager was, however, polite and recognising Sir Richard, was prepared to be helpful. Richard explained that he was thinking of covering his garage floor and thought that a heavy duty lino might do — the sort of stuff they once used to cover the decks of ships. A friend had given him this sample. The manager was willing to indulge the whims of titled clients. "No, we have nothing like that in stock. It's heavy commercial grade stuff supplied mainly to shops and offices. I could get it for you; take a while, I'm afraid."

"Well I would like it quickly if possible. Do you know any other shop I might try?"

The manager was feeling the effects of the recession and was clearly reluctant to give custom to his rivals. He relented however, "You might try 'Hardmans'. They're in a small way of business but they do office floor coverings. Out on the industrial estate." Richard thanked the manager, expressed an interest in some Chinese carpets of hideous design which he thought he might need in the future and left the shop.

The industrial estate had been established by the District Council some ten years earlier. It had been an economic disaster. The official charged with supervising the leasing of the buildings, had little knowledge of commerce and moreover disapproved of all forms of private enterprise. The rents had been fixed far too high and there had been many bankruptcies among the tenants. Several of the small factories were unoccupied and vandalised. Hardmans, was surviving. The small warehouse was at the further end of the estate. A red-painted door was marked 'office' and behind a desk a young woman was manicuring her fingernails. She knew nothing about the lino. She only did the books. Mr Ferdinand would know: he was in the warehouse.

Richard made his way to the back of the building, stumbling over rolls of carpet and piles of matting. Mr Ferdinand was very helpful. He was a cheerful Cockney who might have been the model for the car dealer immortalised by Mr George Cole. He could certainly get Sir Richard some lino like that; cheap too. He had special suppliers! He did not actually say that it 'fell off the back of a lorry' but there was just a ghost of a wink! "I'll place my order when I've got the exact measurements. Have you supplied much of this to local people? I mean does it wear well?"

"I've sold acres of it squire. Never had a complaint. Sold it to lots of shops and offices. The Council had a whole lot about ten years ago."

"Which Council, the County?"

"No, the District. Then I heard they threw it all out when they did the redecoration. It wasn't half worn but they wanted those carpet tile things. More money than sense, but then it isn't their money is it? Rates, Poll Tax, Council Tax — it's all the same. Wait a minute, you're standing for the Council. I'll vote for you if you're against all this waste. Not one of them knows what it's like running a business."

Richard felt that Mr Ferdinand might be a better candidate for Local Government office than himself. He had a forceful, natural eloquence. Resisting the offer of the greatest bargain ever known in carpets, "Wilton type, cancelled export order, unrepeatable," he returned to his car.

Back at the flat, Richard opened a can of soup, prepared his solitary lunch and thought over the problem. The piece of lino had certainly come from the roll that Sam had appropriated.

It was equally certain that the roll was one of those thrown out after the refurbishment of the Council offices. Richard was fairly sure that he knew what the roll had been used for.

It was also a hundred to one that the users had been persons connected with the District Council offices. Persons, because obviously there must have been more than one. Again he felt the need to talk to Polk but then again, he felt he could not face the Sergeant's contempt for interfering amateurs. He needed a Watson.

He did not find his Watson but he got Mrs Oldrieve. After lunch the acting 'chair' telephoned. She was she said, worried about his election. Could she do anything to help? Could she talk to him? The Conservative group had met and they all felt this election was vital. A few more Liberal Democrats and the Party would lose control. Richard asked her to tea. As she was free that afternoon she would call about four.

The only biscuits in his kitchen cupboard were decidedly damp and he had no cake. Hastily tidying his living room first, he made his way to the corner shop. He bought cake, the thinnest sliced bread, a jar of 'Gentlemen's Relish' and a cucumber. As he prepared the sandwiches he remembered that his mother had always removed the crusts when there was company. It seemed such a waste of good bread.

Mrs Oldrieve arrived punctually. It was quite obvious that if the lady had been a betting person she would have given long odds against Richard's chances of success. "You see, Sir Richard, it is not just a matter of pushing pamphlets into letter boxes. Half of them don't get read anyway. Personal canvassing is the thing. A good doorstep manner. Press them — I'm sure you've got lots of charm. Ask about their problems. Listen to them ...." She had much more good advice and Richard doubted that she had ever listened to anyone for more than a moment or two. Also, she obviously did not care for 'Gentleman's Relish'. He passed the cucumber sandwiches. "I was thinking, —" he began, but she cut him short to ask him whether he had thought of holding a public meeting?

"You might get a lot of pensioners coming and you could tell them how much you are in favour of extending the 'meals on wheels' service." Richard had indeed once attended a public meeting to hear the Conservative candidate at the General Election. The chilly church hall had held about twenty people, mainly members of the Anti-Hunting League, protesting at the activities of the candidate who was a well known rider to hounds. It did not seem that Mrs Oldrieve had much faith in the idea for she soon dropped it. "You must have a loudspeaker van going round during the week before the election. The Agent will fix it up and don't forget to get your rosettes."

She looked doubtfully at the sticky cakes her host had provided and during the pause while she made her choice, Richard seized his opportunity. "There was one thing I wanted to ask you. I've been talking to people about the late Colonel Wainwright. He seems to have been disliked by a number of his fellow councillors on both sides of the House, as you might say. But I also wondered if he had also upset some of the more permanent staff; the Officers as they call them? I wouldn't want to make that sort of mistake if I were elected, — I heard — ?"

For once Mrs Oldrieve was listening. When she spoke it was in a harsher tone, the tone she used when chairing difficult meetings. "We have a splendid set of officers — really dedicated people. I have the greatest confidence in them from Neville Gutteridge down to the humblest Clerical Assistant. I will not listen to any criticism of these hard-working public servants. It is our duty as councillors to support them in every way and to give them the best possible working conditions."

"Of course. I'm sure I agree with you. I've only met Mr Gutteridge you know and the people in the office where you get the car park vouchers — they all seem very pleasant."

"They are loyal public servants and you must not listen to foolish gossip. They are there to carry out the policy of the elected representatives. Colonel Wainwright did not quite understand the proper relationship."

"So, there were difficulties?"

"No of course not. No difficulties. We all work together smoothly, as you will find out."

Mrs Oldrieve was not going to say any more. Her manner had changed and Richard felt that she was had become less keen to see the new candidate elected. They chatted uneasily for a little longer and the tea-party ended. Why had the lady been so disturbed?

Chapter 19

That evening Sir Richard sat in his armchair going over the case. He could see another suggestion of a motive. Tomorrow he would look again into those piles of minutes in the public library. The problem of how the body got into the park seemed to be capable of solution. Why hadn't Polk and others thought of it? The time of death and the nature of it was known but what had the deceased Colonel been doing between leaving home and his death?

He opened the neat folder of notes on the case which he had kept and read again the report on the Coroner's inquest. 'Death occurred approximately twenty four hours before the body had been examined, possibly only eighteen.' The doctor had been unwilling to commit himself. That meant that death had occurred during the afternoon or evening of the 20th January. The Colonel had last been seen alive by his wife when she dropped him at the station forecourt for the 11.10. What had happened to him during the next few hours?

The doorbell rang. It was Sam. Sam was dressed in his best suit and sat nervously on the edge of Richard's sofa. Remembering that the dustman disapproved of strong drink, Richard persuaded him to take a cup of coffee. He sipped his Gold Blend appreciatively. "I've asked all the lads about those rolls of lino. There were five or six of them put out behind the Council offices. In that yard at the back. We collected from there on the Friday after we picked up the one by the bottle bank."

"That would be the 25th?"

"I suppose so. None of the gang wanted the old lino so it went to the tip along with the rest of the load. Buried deep now."

"What is the yard like?"

"It's just used for the rubbish skips. They used to put a few staff cars in there but now they've got the new car park, they don't need to."

"Is it overlooked from the buildings?"

"There might be one or two windows you could see it from. Never been inside those offices at the back. It's very dark in that yard with all those trees, specially in winter."

Richard lay back in his chair to consider. It was then that he got the great surprise. Sam put down his coffee cup and looked hard at him. "I reckon you think that the body was rolled up in one of those pieces of lino," he said slowly. "That's what I thought when you came to my place. It would be a good way to move it. If a copper saw them he'd only tell them not to leave it lying there; that's if he even bothered!"

Richard was about to say 'How on earth did you work that out?' when he paused. What a patronising attitude. Why shouldn't a dustman think clearly? He himself had taken a week to figure it out. The man was no fool; after all he had a pretty intelligent daughter.

"I'm going to tell you Sam what I think about the whole affair. I know you'll keep it to yourself. The police officer I told you about thinks I'm crazy so I don't want to say anything to him yet. You see, I've always been interested in criminal investigation; read lots of books about it and having all this time on my hands now ..."

"I heard about all your money and that. It was in the local paper."

"Yes, worst luck! You should have seen the begging letters! Well first I asked people on the Council if they knew of anyone who had a grudge against the Colonel."

"Is that why you're standing in the election?" Again Richard was surprised at Sam's perception. "Well yes, in a way. I thought that another councillor might have hated the Colonel because he opposed a pet scheme and for personal reasons. That was all nonsense. I looked a complete idiot when the police followed it up!"

"Any dustman might have a motive for doing him in. He was the one who wanted all this privatisation. Pushed it through. Mind you, none of the gang would go in for violence. I won't say they're all angels and one or two have had a bit of trouble with the law. Pinching petrol would be about the worst but never any violence." Sam was becoming interested. "No I don't think it was anyone who works outside."

"People in the office?"

"Well, maybe. There's a lot more to find out. You've helped me a lot already. Tell you what though. There's another matter to be cleared up. Do you know anyone who works on the railway. In this area, of course?"

Sam knew several. His brother-in-law had been a signalman until the system was computerised and now was doing clerical work in the Regional Office in Portborough. "What about the people at Bridgeminster station?"

"Not really. Only old Charlie. Everybody knows him, of course." Charlie was a very eccentric porter whose quips and sallies had acquired some local fame. "There's a man in our road who works at Bushwell station but I only know him to pass the time of day."

Bushwell was the first station on the up line to London. Richard rose and took a railway timetable from the bookcase. It told him that the 11.10 from Bridgeminster stopped at Bushwell and passengers had to change there for the fast train from the coast line. There was a wait of five minutes.

"What's the name of your friend, the one at Bushwell?"

"Buckridge, but he's no friend. I don't know him at all really and to tell you the truth I don't think he's quite, er ....., he and his wife have the most awful rows. He has three very scruffy kids — disgusting how some people live."

"I quite agree. Still, he might know something. You see Sam, I reckon the Colonel got on that train but I don't believe he reached London. Now if he didn't, he must have got off somewhere and it might have been Bushwell. The next stop after that is ....." Just here Richard paused to consult the timetable. "The next stop is Marwell Green twenty minutes on. He'd have been on the platform for four or five minutes. Someone may have persuaded him to abandon his journey and return to Bridgeminster."

"Why should they do that?"

"They wanted to get him somewhere quiet. The time would be about right. He was killed sometime during the afternoon — probably. If your man was on the platform that morning, he may have seen someone talking to the Colonel. Perhaps he was persuaded to abandon his journey and went somewhere with his murderer."

"Kidnapped like?"

"Well abducted, I suppose. Perhaps they told him that he was needed elsewhere. That his wife was ill or something of that sort."

"Wouldn't he have rung up?"

"Well we don't know what the story was but if your porter chap saw him leave the station, it must have been to a car that took him somewhere. That would be important evidence."

"I don't see how I can ask him all this, not knowing him properly! Didn't the police ought to question him? I wouldn't think that Buckridge, (Alf Buckridge is his name, I remember), is particularly bright. It's more than two months. Nobody would remember that long."

Richard felt that Sam was not particularly keen on getting involved any further in the matter. He tried another approach. "This is a nasty crime, Sam. Somebody bashed the poor old chap's head in, in cold blood. Public duty to try and find out who did it." The dustman was coming to a decision. "How do you suggest I get to ask him?"

"Get to talk to him in the pub, say — buy him a drink or two and bring up the subject of the murder. I suppose people still talk about it locally."

"I'm not one for pubs. Too busy with the pigeons. I suppose he drinks at the 'Prince Albert', that's our local. I could take the missus down there Friday night. They have one of these quiz evenings."

"Good idea. Now look Sam, you'll have to make up some story as to why you want to know. Say it's a bet you're having with a policeman friend. People will always help with a bet. You can think of something."

Sam was obviously troubled but he said, "Well Sir, I owe you a favour so I'll have a try. Give me a week to ten days. What they're going to say when they see me in the 'Prince Albert' I can't think. The wife will take a glass of sherry at times though." The dustman rose to leave.

"You'll have to spend a bit Sam." Richard took out his wallet and took out some notes.

"No need of that, sir."

"No, I insist. Treat it as expenses. Keep a record of what you spend if you like and give Mrs Absey a good time." Sam took the money reluctantly.

As he saw his visitor out Richard could not help remembering that, before he came into his fortune, he had not realised how difficult it was for rich men to get rid of their money!

Chapter 20

The next morning Richard drank coffee in the lounge of the 'Angel Hotel', dark and filled with fake antiques, reflecting as he sipped that he was behaving more and more like the elderly retired citizens of Bridgeminster who filled the room.

At the next table sat Mrs Oldrieve. Richard rose to greet her with the old-world courtesy that had so amused the Progressive women teachers at Alderman Grimshaw Comprehensive. She asked him to join her and they chatted about Council affairs and the coming election. "I'm having terrible problems today," she complained. "Did you know that I'm County Chairman of the Women's Institute? They keep ringing me up with their problems. I had two branch secretaries call me this morning complaining that their speakers have let them down. How can I find speakers for them with all my commitments? Now, wait a minute, I'm sure you could give an interesting talk about something and they'd love a baronet!"

"Oh but really, I don't think I could. I've no experience."

"You don't need experience, just charm. Now let me see. Would you rather South Benham or Hangleton? They're both very keen branches." She took out her diary. "Hangleton want a speaker next Wednesday fortnight. I know it's short notice but I'm sure you can cope. South Benham is in a fortnight's time, you could do that too. The same talk would do and they pay the speaker you know. Ten or fifteen pounds is the usual and you'd get mileage allowance if you use your car. But I suppose ......"

Richard was still terrified at the thought of talking to a Women's Institute but the name 'Hangleton' made him pause. Hadn't Polk said that Mrs Wainwright had not reported her husband missing that night because she had been at a WI party and thought he might have stayed in London? It was a dreadful prospect but detectives have to face fearful odds. "Well I suppose I might. What could I talk about? I read English Lit. at university but there's not much else I know about."

"Oh good. Will you do both?" Richard was firm. "No, please let me see how it goes first. Hangleton's a little village. There won't be a large audience I suppose? I'm free on that Wednesday but I'm not sure about the next two weeks." This was quite untrue!

"Right, have you got your diary? Here's the secretary's phone number; Miss Puttock. No she's very deaf and not too good on the phone. Ring the President; that's Mrs Wainwright, the Colonel's widow. She's a charming person, you'll like her. She was a good deal younger than her husband you know and quite modern in her thinking. It's a pity she hasn't thought of coming on the Council. She does a lot of church work too."

"I'll ring her today Mrs Oldrieve."

"Oh do call me Helen. All my friends do. It's so kind of you to help out, particularly when you are so busy with the election."

Richard had done nothing about the election. He hadn't knocked on a single door in Bridgeminster South. The pile of pamphlets had not been touched. He felt guilty. Mrs Oldrieve gathered up her shopping and handbag. "I suppose you could talk to them about Literature," she conceded doubtfully, "but they are country folk out there. Farmers' wives some of them. Not D H Lawrence of course, or that man who wrote those funny books without sentences, 'Molly something..... Richard had not thought of talking about the works of James Joyce. "You might try the Brontes though or Jane Austen, they'll have heard of them."

Mrs Oldrieve left, and Richard paid his bill and followed her out into Union Street. Turning left he crossed the road to W H Smith. As he paid for his weekly copy of the 'Spectator', he found himself next to the sturdy figure of Detective Sergeant James Polk, who was similarly engaged in collecting his copy of 'The Stage'. They had not met for some time.

"Hello James! Off duty? Come and have a drink. How is the new play going?" As usual, the new play was not going well. The leading lady was being difficult and the tickets weren't selling. Richard sipped a half pint of bitter while the detective consumed several whiskies. They sat in the far corner of the saloon bar of 'The Phoenix', an old fashioned pub that had not yet introduced either a juke-box or a fruit machine. After Polk's third whisky, Richard judged that he might be persuaded to disclose something.

"How is the murder investigation going?" he asked, with what he imagined sounded like careless indifference. "Cor, you're not still on about that? For God's sake don't have any more ideas.

That last one caused enough trouble. It's left on the file, as you might say. Every line of enquiry led nowhere. Pages of notes, statements and nothing to go on. No motive either."

"I've had another idea about motive."

"Well, don't tell me: I don't want to know. I suppose you think it was the Mafia behind it. Wainwright was Bridgeminster's drug baron, was it? You read too many detective stories." There was a pause as Polk drained his glass. "Alright, I'll buy it. What was the motive then?"

"No. I won't tell you. I could be wrong. But I'll bet you a bottle of that whisky you liked the other day; that in a way, there's money involved in it."

"Money? His money was in his pocket. He wasn't robbed."

"Not in that sense. You think it over. I must be off. Got to get something for lunch. You married men get it cooked for you!" Polk, was going through a difficult time with his wife. He was not getting many hot dinners and did not find this funny. "It's the canteen for me today — she's out. Money eh? Much money?"

"Yes, quite a bit: in a way, as I said."

"Well carry on, Sherlock. Thought any more about joining the Specials?" Polk returned to his duties but he did put the idea tentatively to Inspector Morris that afternoon.

"Could there have been something financial at the bottom of it? After all he was on the way to see his stockbroker that very morning? I thought perhaps ....." Inspector Morris did not want to know what his Sergeant thought. He told him to get on with investigating the recent epidemic of frauds on elderly persons, by door-to-door salesmen. The Park Murder Case was dead!

Chapter 21

Richard ate a rather tough pork chop with tinned potatoes. While he ate, he planned his visit to Mrs Wainwright. He would telephone and ask to call to discuss the talk to the Women's Institute. With luck she would ask him to tea. Then he would subtly bring up the subject of her husband's murder. It would need lots of tact. How could he explain to her that he was trying to investigate the crime? She would be bound to think it ungentlemanly.

As it turned out it was quite simple. After lunch he phoned the lady and she invited him to call that afternoon. "After all, there's not much time before the next meeting for you to prepare your talk. Mrs Oldrieve rang me and told me that you were prepared to come! The members will be pleased."

She welcomed him warmly. A small, neat, smiling lady. A 'real lady' was Richard's assessment. There was tea, with the thinnest of cucumber sandwiches, in her pleasant sitting room, the walls hung with faded photographs of her late husband during his military career. "What are you going to talk about?" she asked. "It's very brave of you. Mrs Oldrieve tells me that you haven't done this sort of thing before."

Richard took the plunge. "You see, Mrs Wainwright, I have always been interested in historical mysteries. I wonder if your WI ladies would like to hear a talk about the Tichbourne Case? The missing heir and the false claimant? I've been reading a lot about it and it took place in the next county so there is a sort of local interest."

"They won't mind what you talk about. We've never had a real live Baronet before, but it sounds very interesting. Our speakers usually talk for about forty minutes. Can you manage that? Did they find the missing heir?"

Richard gave her an outline of the great Victorian mystery. "They'll be fascinated. Poor Maurice loved to read mystery stories, then he left us with a mystery of his own."

"A terrible tragedy." Richard tried his best to be conventionally concerned.

"Yes. I'm beginning to make a new life though, he wouldn't have wanted me to pine."

"I read all about it in the papers and I happen to know one of the police officers who was appointed on the case."

"Was that Inspector Morris? Such a nice man. He was so nice about it."

"I know Sergeant Polk. Perhaps he didn't come to see you. I know that he was very distressed that they failed to make an arrest. They thought it would be quite straightforward, at first."

"So did I. There was that letter you know. It must have been meant to lure him up to London but he didn't get to London, did he?"

"No, but I think that he got on the train and then got off again, probably at the next station. I think that someone contacted him and persuaded him to return to Bridgeminster."

Mrs Wainwright put down her cup of tea and eyed Richard thoughtfully. "I suppose this is just another mystery you are interested in. I'm afraid I cannot see it as just a problem looking for a solution. We were married for more than forty years and were very close, you know."

It was as near an expression of emotion as the Colonel's lady was likely to show. Her visitor felt he was getting out of his depth. He swallowed half a cupful of tea before replying, "I thought you might take it like that. I can't help taking an interest. It's a sort of — well not hobby exactly — a sort of ...." his voice tailed away.

"No you don't understand. I'm not offended. I've had enough time since it happened and justice ought to be done. The police seem to have given up. The last time I saw the Inspector he had — what is it you call them — no new lines of enquiry."

"Mrs Wainwright, I believe that I have a sort of theory about your husband's murder. I may be all wrong and the police would probably say it's all nonsense but ......"

"Have you told the police, your friend the Sergeant?"

"I put my first ideas to him but they were all wrong. Since then I have found out one or two things and I believe I know the motive."

"The police made some horrible suggestions about motive. It was all nonsense. Maurice wasn't that sort of man at all."

"I know; they have to ask those questions."

"What do you think was the motive then?"

"I'd rather not go into details as I said. I could be wrong again but I believe it was something to do with his work as Chairman of the Council."

Mrs Wainwright did not seem as surprised as Richard expected. "Oh they were always having terrible rows. All Councils are like that. I was on the Parish council for four years but I gave it up. Too much bickering. No harm meant though — well, not much. It wouldn't lead to murder would it?"

"There was a murder!"

Mrs Wainwright made a decision. "You don't fool me. I suppose you agreed to talk to our WI so that you could ask me questions. I remember now. It was in the papers. You caught a burglar. What do you want to know? I don't know much about his Council work. He knew it bored me — all that sort of thing."

"No, not about that. About that morning, when you drove your husband to the station."

"I told the police all I knew."

"Yes but I haven't read the evidence you gave. My detective friend only gave me an outline. They're not allowed to show it to outsiders."

"I took him to the station. I didn't park the car but just dropped him at the entrance and drove away. I was thinking of all the things I had to do for the WI party that evening."

"Was he quite cheerful that morning?"

"Oh yes perfectly. He was cross about having to go to London at breakfast time but he cheered up. I think he intended to stay at his club, then he wouldn't have had to come to the party you see. Husbands are invited! That is why I wasn't worried when he didn't get back."

"Was he carrying anything?"

"Only his small briefcase. I suppose he took some papers for the stockbrokers. They couldn't have been important because his solicitor didn't find that anything important was missing. Certificates and so on were all in the bank."

"One more question. Your husband got out of the car and walked into the station. Was there any one about that you might have recognised? Mrs Wainwright thought for a long moment before answering. "They asked me that and I said, 'No' ... I didn't recognise anyone, I'm quite certain but ......"

"Something happened?"

"I don't know. It's so long ago. I'm afraid I do not have a good visual memory. I remember things people say but I don't remember their faces. My eyesight, though is very good for my age."

"But there was something?"

"It's all so vague. Just a glimpse. He was walking towards those doors and then — I had the impression — I think, that someone turned away as if to avoid seeing him. You know, they used to call it 'cutting a man'."

"Was it a man or a woman? "I suppose it was a man, I don't know. Something grey, — a grey suit or a grey overcoat — tallish I think and thin."

"Do you suppose someone was watching for him?"

"I don't know. I wasn't really looking at all. Just an impression. A dark coat, an office suit you know, something like that." She paused. "Were you expecting me to say that someone was watching?"

"Well yes. I thought it possible." Richard did not want to be asked any more questions. "I have taken up too much of your time already. May I come again if I think of anything else?"

"Of course. It must seem strange to you but I don't seem to feel strongly about finding the murderer. It wouldn't bring him back. I have never thought it right to look for revenge."

Richard was embarrassed. Was it really possible that she should be so unmoved? He thanked her for the tea. "Well you can't get out of giving your talk anyway — seven thirty for eight, in the Village Hall. There's always a certain amount of business to get through before the speaker comes on. Mrs Parminter will be your hostess and meet you at the door. We leave a car park space for the speaker. We usually give the speaker his fee and a mileage allowance but ..."

"Oh no — no fee."

"Miss Braithwaite will be pleased. She's our Treasurer. Goodbye, Sir Richard."

Chapter 22

Sunday morning was a sunny spring day. At ten o-clock the infernal jangling of the Cathedral bells had just ceased calling the faithful to prayer and Richard was spreading a new and expensive brandy-flavoured marmalade on his toast. After all, he reflected he could afford such luxuries now. The first mouthful told him that he should have stayed loyal to Coopers Oxford. It was rather nasty. The doorbell rang. It was Sam.

"Just finishing breakfast Sam. Sit down and have some coffee. Or would you rather have tea? Have a slice of toast and try this marmalade I've bought. I'm not sure I like it." Sam accepted coffee and spread the confection doubtfully across a slice of toast. "Funny sort of taste sir. My missus makes a big boiling every winter. Would you like a pot?"

"I'd love some. Don't forget. What do you have to tell me?"

Sam believed in first things first. He pulled out a bit of paper. "I have spent £32.75 already, Sir. That's a balance due of £27.25. I've got it here." He pulled out a small plastic bag of notes and coins. "Keep it for now Sam. I'm going to have some more work for you soon. What did you find out?"

"Well Sir, I spent two evenings in that pub. The first time I bought three lemonade shandies for myself and two sherries for my Emma. Oh and two chicken and chips in the basket. It's all written down."

"Did you ...?"

"No sir, he never came that night. I asked around and they said he usually came on Fridays but he didn't."

"Then you went again on Saturday?"

"Right Sir, and very full it was. Noisy too. Gave my Emma quite a headache. She stuck it out. She had spaghetti and I had ..."

"Don't worry about the expenses Sam, we'll sort it out later. Did Buckridge turn up?"

"Yes Sir and I got talking to him.

I had to make up a bit of a story though to get him to talk. His name's Alf. His mates call him that anyway. It's short for Alfred."

"What did you tell him?"

"A real 'cock and bull' story! I said I'd met a gent on my rounds who was a retired copper, from the Met. He'd had a bet with a pal that he could find out who done the local murder. I said the gent didn't think much of the local bobbies and wanted to show them up. I said he was trying to get information about the railway journey the old Colonel was making. I don't know whether Buckeridge believed the story — I wouldn't have!"

"Did he talk?"

"Yes. He did, in a way. I bought him, (here Sam consulted his piece of paper), four pints of best bitter and what they call shorts, gin, it was. Total cost ....."

"What did he tell you?"

"He was on the platform that morning, that's for certain. He remembers because that was the day the snow started. He says that very few people ever get off the train there at that time. They're all going up to London.

"Did anybody get off?"

"He can't say for sure. But he did say one thing."

"Go on."

"There was someone who came onto the station with a platform ticket. A man he says, who walked up and down as if he were waiting for someone off the train. He says, that the chap kept to the far end — not under the sheltered part. That's what he thought was funny."

"Could he describe him?"

"No just an ordinary sort of person. Not a working man though. With a hat, he says. A big man."

"Did he see him leave the platform?"

"No he didn't. The other porter was taking the tickets and Alf had to collect some parcels that needed to go on the train."

"Did you ask him to keep quiet about all this?"

"Well I did but I don't suppose he will. He might not remember much though. He was still drinking after we left. He's got a reputation for drink."

Richard pondered for a moment or two. "You've done a splendid job, Sam. What you tell me fits in with the theory I've been working on. Somebody met that train at Bushwell and got the Colonel to get off. Then he was taken somewhere. The question is — where?"

"He was going to London, wasn't he?"

"Yes he was, but someone might have pretended to give him an urgent message. A story to persuade him to return to Bridgeminster. Was there a car parked in the station yard?"

"I didn't ask him, but there is a car park there. A lot of people go from there to London every day. Commuters."

"Could you have another go at him Sam? I'd like to know about cars. If someone just stopped to collect the Colonel off the train, they might not have used the proper car park but just stopped briefly in the station yard. I suppose there is a taxi rank at Bushwell?"

"Just for one or two cabs. Buckridge wouldn't have seen cars parked if he was on the platform."

Sam was clearly not relishing the prospect of another evening in the Prince Albert. "I'll try him if you like Sir, but I don't know what my Emma will say. I can't go on my own; not knowing the regulars, like."

"You're a hero Sam and so is Mrs Absey and don't get her spaghetti. The best steak there is in that pub — all on expenses, mind!"

"She's gone nearly vegetarian. It's Helen. She's the younger. She's joined the Green Party and showed Emma pictures of how they slaughter bullocks. Put her off meat it has!"

"Well give her a good time and spend as much as you like."

Sam stood up. "What sort of car had you in mind?"

"Oh nothing in particular. No sensible criminal would use a bright coloured sports car or something noticeable."

"Could it be a van or a truck?"

Richard paused. "You know Sam, you keep getting bright ideas. I never thought of that. Yes, I think perhaps it could have been a van."

Before leaving Sam made another effort to sort out the matter of his expenses and was reluctantly persuaded to accept a further twenty pound note. He even asked if he would be liable to pay tax on the money he had spent on entertainment. It occurred to Richard that had Sam been given the opportunities he might well have become Britain's first entirely honest merchant banker!

Chapter 23

It would be an exaggeration to say that Richard Smith solved the Abbey Park Murder Mystery during the following night, but after Sam had left, he sat in front of his gas fire for some time. It was cold for April. He thought he had worked out the motive: the method too was becoming clear but who had had that motive? Who had used that method? Somewhere there must be evidence that would point to the murderers. What a fool he would look if he raised suspicions against an innocent person.

He remembered the fiasco of the Palmers. Polk had kept quiet about that. He wouldn't be so generous a second time. Then he remembered what had led him to think foolishly that the Palmers had anything to do with it. It was those minutes of the Council meeting filed away in the Public Library. He had wrongly thought that they would reveal deep hatreds that could lead to murder among the local Councillors. They might equally reveal hatreds of a different nature.

The next morning Richard was at the Library at opening time. All that morning he read through the tedious records of Committee meetings made during the year before Colonel Wainwright's death. Wainwright as Chairman was a member of every Committee. It seemed that he attended almost all of them!

In May of last year, the Colonel had incurred the wrath of all the Progressive members of the Housing Committee by arguing that the policy of allotting Council Flats to unmarried mothers was calculated to encourage fornication. He had only been silenced by the clerk reminding the Committee that they were compelled by law to following Government guidelines in the matter.

He had offended all the members of the Tourism Development Sub-Committee by flatly stating that there were too many foreigners in Bridgeminster and that the crime rate was linked to the presence of aliens! The Environmental Health Committee had been outraged by the Colonel's opposition to providing subsidised Contraceptive Vending Machines in the local College of Further Education. So it went on. Richard took his lunch at the Taj Mahal Indian restaurant and returned to his search.

For five more days, Richard sat at a Library table reading the minutes of the District Council. Each evening he read through the notes he had made. They amounted to very little. It was on the sixth day, the Saturday, that he found something. There had been a Special Committee established to consider Administrative Reorganisation. The Colonel had chaired it and all the Chairmen of Committees had been members. Gutteridge, the Chief Executive, had been its Secretary. It had met seven or eight times in the months before the Colonel's death. The minutes of this Committee were sketchy: it was not always easy to discover the attitudes of the members. Gutteridge, it was clear, was opposed to all change. He clearly believed that the administrative set-up he presided over was the best organised in the best of all possible worlds!

The December meeting seemed to have been particularly acrimonious. The Colonel had expressed the opinion that most of the Council's business could be handled by a couple of reasonably efficient orderly room clerks. Gutteridge had gallantly defended the honour of his loyal, over worked and conscientious subordinates. It must have been quite a meeting.

At the end of the report was a brief note, 'The Committee agreed to investigate the possibility of giving the work of the Parks and Open Spaces Department to private contractors and merging the Housing Department and the Department of Environmental Health. A further meeting in February was agreed.' Richard gave the file back to the Librarian. It was what he had been looking for.

Chapter 24

The next day was the Wednesday of the WI meeting. Richard's evenings had been spent on reading up on the great Victorian 'cause celebre'. His first draft of notes had filled a dozen sheets of foolscap but he remembered that Mrs Wainwright had said that they expected their speakers to talk for thirty or forty minutes. Several revisions later, he was moderately satisfied.

It was a warm evening when he parked in the carefully marked space at the Village Hall. Mrs Parminter wearing a badge identifying her as 'hostess', took charge of him. "We just have a little business to attend to before your talk Sir Richard. Would you like to sit here until the President gets through it?"

The hard tubular chair was most uncomfortable. Richard sat politely through a report on the Regional conference, the Agenda for the next Group Meeting, the Secretary's report, the Committee's plans for participation in the Village Flower Festival and, interminably, the Treasurer's Statement of Accounts! About this last there was some acrimony.

Unfriendly questions came from several members and the President was forced to intervene. Richard noted that Mrs Wainwright was a competent Chairman: doubtless, she had had years of experience in running a Regimental Welfare Committee. After some forty minutes the business affairs came to an end with the Secretary reading every word of the Branch correspondence. Richard mounted the platform and was introduced.

The 'Tichborne Case' makes a good story and a man who has taught English Literature to backward readers ought to be a good story-teller. The heir to a fortune who escapes overseas after an unhappy love affair. His ship missing and he is presumed dead. Then, years later, the appearance of the claimant from Australia and the astonishing gullibility of so many Hampshire gentlemen in recognising him as genuine.

Then, the known facts about Orton, the butcher's boy from Wapping and the long struggle in the courts. The claimant had actually visited Bridgeminster to hold one of his fund-raising meetings at the Angel Hotel: there were still people in the city who had Tichborne bonds among their family heirlooms.

It went down very well and the applause was genuine. They would have enjoyed any talk from a young baronet but this one was full of human interest!

Afterwards, coffee and cakes were served. The cakes were very much better than those which Richard was used to buying at 'Pam's Pantry' or even the up-market 'Patisserie Normande', a new venture by a failed property developer named Gribble. It was over coffee that Mrs Wainwright was able to have a private word with the guest speaker.

"I thought I'd write to you, but I wasn't sure until today. I told you that I saw someone that morning, at the station when he got out of the car. It came to me this morning just after I woke up. It isn't that I can remember who it was: but I think it was — someone slightly familiar. Someone I'd met before — somewhere. I've been going over it in my mind — no, it's no good asking me any questions — but it was someone — slightly familiar, and it was a man — I'm quite sure of that.

The secretary was bearing down on them with a fresh plate of cakes and Mrs Wainwright abruptly changed the subject. There were other ladies wishing to talk to their almost-noble guest and it was some time before Richard was able to get away. It had not been so terrible after all and Mrs Wainwright's bit of evidence certainly fitted.

If only she had not sent him away with the assurance that she would tell other WI Presidents about his wonderful talk and asked him what other topics he could speak on. Back at the flat, he went through it all again. Reflecting that affluence led to temptation and that his mother would have disapproved, he poured himself a weak whisky and water, taking care to use the expensive brand that Polk had scorned. Someone had to use it up.

He was beginning to get it clear. There must have been someone at the station and it was easy to see why he was there. It had always been certain that two persons were involved in the killing and they must have shared the motive. One at Bushwell station with a story ready to persuade the Colonel to leave the train; the other at Bridgeminster to telephone his accomplice and confirm that their victim had left; there were phone boxes at both stations. It was complicated. Surely they could have thought of something simpler?

At this point Richard paused. Until this evening, he realised, he had been treating the whole affair as a sort of game, an intellectual exercise. No more real than an attempt to solve the problems left unexplained in the Tichborne Case. Now, for the first time he saw the horror of it all. Two men, desperate to protect themselves, luring an old man to some spot where they could beat him to death. It was not nice.

It also occurred to him that such men might feel themselves threatened if they knew someone was on the verge of uncovering their plot. He shivered slightly and finished his whisky. Before he went to bed, he telephoned Sam. Sam was out at a meeting of his Pigeon Fancier's Club but the next day was Sam's day off so Mrs Absey promised that she would get him to call round.

Next morning Richard ate his bacon and eggs glumly. He had overcooked the eggs and the bacon was greasy. He had never mastered the art of producing crisp bacon. Perhaps, he thought, he was becoming over pre-occupied with the park mystery. Again the thought came of how nice it would be if he had someone to cook his breakfast and sit opposite him in a quilted housecoat like the one his mother used to wear, only more glamorous of course! Someone who he would be able to discuss things with.

Such dreams may be perfectly normal in a shy young bachelor but they do not help him to order his thoughts clearly. When Sam rang the doorbell, Richard was still somewhat distrait.

Sam was wearing his day-off clothes — a neat tweed sports jacket with corduroy trousers. His tie bore a pattern of flying pigeons. He sipped his coffee, explaining that he was trying to get his Emma to change to this 'Continental Blend' but she was resisting the experiment. "She doesn't like changes you know." The dustman believed in doing things decently and in order and the preliminaries were gone through.

After his second cup of coffee he seemed ready for business and Richard began. "Now Sam I want you to follow all this closely. You worked out the way the murder was done quicker than I did and I think you have got a clue as to my idea of the motive. Since I saw you last I have made some discoveries. You have worked for the Council for years. What do you know about the Housing Department and the Parks Department?"

"I wouldn't know much about Housing. Now that half the Council houses have been sold off they don't have so much to do. I bought mine myself. Good bargain. Of course we do the Council estates on our rounds. My gang does the West Grove estate."

"And the Parks?"

"Mr Garrowby is Head of that. They don't like him. I know Dennis Broadstairs — he works on the Sports Grounds. He says Garrowby is all 'red-tape' — niggling."

"Who is Head of Housing?"

"That's Mr Henshaw. He's a younger man. I only saw him once and that's when we signed the papers for our house. Bit of a lad they say. You know, one for the ladies! My youngest did a temporary job clerking with the Council before she went to College. He would always be pinching the girls: that sort of thing. My Helen wouldn't stand for it though. Her mother always warned her about men like that. Come to think of it I heard something about him recently. Divorce, I think it was."

"What about Garrowby?"

"He's much older — fifties I'd say. He lives up Curtis Avenue. We used to do that road and he was always complaining about something or other. Said we broke his side gate once. Half off its hinges it was! His wife's an invalid."

"Where does Henshaw live?"

"That I don't know but I can easily find out." The dustman looked worried, "You don't think it was anything to do with those two do you?" Richard paused, "Sam, I found something out this week. There was a Committee, a special Committee to plan the re-organisation. Colonel Wainwright was on it. They were thinking of closing down the Parks Department and combining the Housing and Health Departments. You see what that would mean?"

"That they would lose their jobs. But they'd get compensation wouldn't they — redundancy money. Some of my lads did alright when the new system came in."

"What if they had heavy commitments? You say Henshaw had a divorce? And Garrowby an invalid wife?" It was a long moment before Sam replied. "I don't like it, Sir Richard, accusing people: I mean. I don't believe they'd murder an old man like that just for their jobs. Nobody would."

"Tell me Sam, have you ever been out of work?"

"Twice. Only for a few weeks though."

"How did you manage."

"Emma's a good manager. No butter, only marge. Sausages for Sunday dinner instead of a joint. I sold some pigeons."

"But what if you'd had a mortgage, insurance and medical bills, and hire purchase on the car and perhaps another family to support? You've read it in the papers about people losing their homes through unemployment?"

This time there was an even longer silence. Sam drank the last dregs of his cold coffee. "What do you want me to do?" he asked weakly. Richard stood up and took a folded map from the book shelf. "This is an ordnance survey map of the Bridgeminster district. Here's the inner city area and here's Bushwell. That line is the main road between the two. Now what I want to know is this. Is there, near that road, a Council Housing estate or any other buildings owned by the District Council? Preferably somewhere quiet away from other buildings?"

Sam poured over the map. "There's the Depot here. You turn up the main road about there." He indicated the lane to the north of the road. "Now nearer Bridgeminster there's the Grendon estate. About twenty houses. They were married quarters when there was an aerodrome at Grendon. It's all gone now and the Council took over the houses. They use them for what they call 'problem families'.

"Are they all occupied?"

"I wouldn't know now. I haven't done collections there for years. There were always one or two empty for doing up 'cos those families usually left them in a bad state when they moved out. Pretty rough, some of them were."

"It sounds the sort of place. If you're free for a bit would you come along?" Sam was still reluctant. "I never meant to get mixed up in this Sir. I wanted to oblige you but shouldn't it be the police?"

"Sam they wouldn't listen yet. You've got a way of seeing into a problem that fits with my way of looking at it. I need your help. I feel like you about it. It's horrible. I didn't realise what it would be like when it came to naming names. I'd be glad if you'd come. And Sam,.....I've talked to his widow. She has a right to know who did it."

"You think that's where they took him?"

"It wouldn't be the depot. I suppose there's always people working there. It would be somewhere quiet and somewhere they'd have the keys to."

"Oh he'd have the keys. Easy for him."

"That's what I thought. Will you come?"

Sam stood up. He said nothing as Richard moved to the door, he followed down the staircase and across the paved area to the block of garages where the Fiesta was kept. The car had not been starting easily and Richard had been gloomily considering the possibility that he might have to get a new one, but this morning it burst into life immediately.

Sam was still silent as they left the city on the Bushwell road. Even a friendly enquiry about his pigeons failed to enliven him.

The Grendon estate was a depressing sight. The houses had been married quarters for the other ranks. Three quarters of a mile down the road the officers' married quarters had been sold to a Property company which had landscaped the area and added some new 'Executive Homes'. These were desirable residences but the Grendon properties were a very sad sight indeed.

Almost all the gardens were weed-filled and littered with old prams, broken toys and bicycles. Across a field could be seen the remains of the old control tower and a few acres of concrete was all that was left of the runways from which the Lancasters and Halifaxes had once lifted off into the night sky. Apart from one or two untidy children playing in the road, none of the problem families was visible. There were however, a surprising number of dangerous-looking dogs!

Chapter 25

The houses were semi-detached. All appeared to be occupied except for one pair at the entrance to the estate. This bore a builder's signboard proclaiming that repairs and renovations were being undertaken by Harris and Hobbs, General Builders and Decorators. Neither Harris nor Hobbs seemed to be in attendance and no van was parked nearby. The gate to the garden was missing and Richard, followed by Sam, walked up the garden path.

Work seemed to have started on the left hand house. The doors and windows frames had recently been repainted and the guttering looked new. Nothing had been done to the other house. Several windows were broken. There was nothing to be seen through the dirty front windows of either house. At the rear it was possible to see into the kitchen. Both were indescribably filthy. In one the occupants must have thrown a lot of soup at the walls. One garden had a very dilapidated shed, its door missing and the windows broken. The floor was strewn with torn newspaper and the plastic chips, used for packing fragile articles.

It was Sam who spotted it. He bent down and picked up a small brown fragment. "Do you reckon it's the same Sir? They must have put the roll in here — the shed's big enough." It was a very small fragment. There was obviously nothing wrong with Sam's eyesight. Very little of the brown surface material remained but it was certainly the same lino that they had both handled. Richard was impressed.

"Were you looking for it Sam?"

"I reckon they must have put the lino in there Sir. It wouldn't be easy to get it into the house; easier for them out there."

Richard found a piece of paper in his pocket and folded it round the scrap of lino. "Of course, it isn't necessarily from the same roll. The housing people might have sent some of the old lino here to be used in the refurbishing. They might not buy new for problem families. You said there was a lot of it."

As they walked down the garden path to the car, Richard saw a curtain move in the house opposite. The house was different from the others. The fences were unbroken and the gate bore the name 'Chatsworth' in plastic lettering. The curtains were lace and a large white Persian cat could be seen keeping a wary eye on the mongrels in the road.

"Do you think we could find an excuse to call on that house Sam?"

"Can't think of one, Sir. You ought to have a clipboard with you. Everyone in the Council offices has one. They'd think you were official then." Richard was continually being impressed by Sam's intelligence. He should have thought of a clipboard.

"Well, we'll have to do without it; here goes." At Richard's knock the door opened instantly but only for a few inches. There was a chain. A small, thin face showed through the crack. Richard gave his most reassuring smile. "Good morning, madam. I hope I'm not intruding. My friend here is interested in one of the two houses opposite and we wondered if you could give us some information about it."

The lady was apparently reassured by Richard's general appearance and decided to remove the chain and open the door. She was about seventy years old, neatly dressed and her grey hair was done in an old fashioned bun. She wore a silver chain round her neck with a crucifix on it. "Is he on the housing list? They won't sell those houses. No-one could get a mortgage in this road, I know."

"Well no. Not exactly. He has a council house but he thinks the country air would suit his — er — pigeons better. I'm sort of advising him." Richard, with a sidelong glance got the impression that Sam was deeply shocked by the duplicity. The lady too, looked doubtful. People obviously did not willingly move to the Grendon estate. But she asked them in.

Her sitting room was incredibly neat. There were antimacassars on the easy chairs and dried flowers arranged in vases. Reproductions of well known paintings, mostly of religious subjects, were on the walls. A knitting machine stood on a small table and the white cat was not friendly.

She was Mrs Mannheim, a widow. Her husband had been a German POW and she had met him when he had worked on her father's farm at the end of the war. He had been a skilled watchmaker and by some clever manipulation of the immigration procedures had managed to return to England to marry her. He had set up in business in Bridgeminster and had done well but died of cancer when he was in his late sixties. They had no children. Sam remembered taking a watch for repairs to Heinrich Mannheim. She was obviously lonely and very willing to talk. She brought them tea and home-made biscuits.

She was surprised that anyone should want to live at Number 2. The O'Shaugnessys had had it with their nine children. There had been trouble with those children. Their mother drank. She admitted that the husband, (if he was her husband), had been good natured but was often away — in gaol. She had very little to do with the other people on the estate. It was all right living here at present as she could still use her bicycle. If her arthritis got worse she would have to try to get a bungalow near the shops.

Richard explained that he was standing for the Council. If he were elected, he would try and do something about the bungalow! Sam looked even more disapproving at this flagrant attempt to offer inducements to a witness. She had heard of Sir Richard and that he was going to be a Councillor. It explained his giving advice to Sam. Obviously Councillors and people of that sort were always interfering in other people's affairs!

Tactfully, Richard brought the conversation back to the subject of Number 2. The O'Shaugnessys had moved out more than a year ago. The Council workers had not boarded up the windows quickly enough and there had been vandalism. She hoped that when the houses were done up there would be some decent tenants. She did not seem optimistic.

Richard took the plunge. Sam was going to get be shocked again! "You said, Sam, that when you last came to see the estate there had been a snowfall and that seemed to put you off. That was January, wasn't it?" Sam duly looked disgusted but Mrs Mannheim was merely puzzled.

"I remember that day. There were several people came there. It was that day when Tibbles wanted to go out in the snow. He'd never seen the snow before being only eighteen months and he looked so funny trying to catch the snowflakes." Sam's conscience was troubling him. "I don't think....." he began.

"Oh no, it couldn't have been that day you came. I saw them in the morning, well before dinner time. A big man and a little man in a dark coat. They came in a green van."

"You had a blue van didn't you Sam?" Sam couldn't bring himself to reply but Mrs Mannheim rattled on. "Yes I do remember. I didn't see them go because I walked to the Post Office to get my pension and when I got back, they were gone."

"Did they come back?"

"I didn't see. I was in this room doing my knitting all the afternoon, I remember because I had that trouble with the Simpson boys at tea time."

"Trouble?"

"They threw snowballs at Tibbles when he went out to do his duties. There wasn't really enough for snowballs. I gave them what for!"

Tibbles, from his place on the window sill, gave a contemptuous look at the company that would discuss such a delicate matter! He was a very well-bred cat.

"Did you see any other visitors that day?"

"Not that I remember. There was a car parked outside there very late one night. It might have been the same night. About that time of year."

"What sort of car?"

"Big, dark and red. What they call an Estate, like my sister's husband's got."

"Mrs Mannheim, could you try to remember?" There's been a lot of interference with Council properties you know and I think the Department would be interested." Mrs Mannheim appeared to accept this explanation. "There was a car. I looked out after I finished watching television. I have the TV in my bedroom since my husband died and I go to bed quite early. It was late; about half past ten, but I can't remember the day."

"What were you watching on TV?"

"It was 'Dad's Army' — a repeat, you know. My husband used to love it. He wasn't really a Nazi but he always thought the British Army was a bit comic! He thought it wasn't really serious about fighting."

"Did you see the car leave?"

"No. It was gone by the morning."

"Can you describe the two men who came that morning?"

"One was a big man. I only saw his back. I think they both had hats on. The small man was in dark clothes like they wear in London."

"Could he have had a bowler hat?"

"Oh I don't know. Not many wear them now."

There was no more to be gleaned from Mrs Mannheim. Richard took his leave promising to do anything in his power about the bungalow. It was all very well for Sam to be contemptuous: after all, Richard could well afford to buy the lady one!

Richard dropped Sam at his home. "Can you possibly spare the time to come round this evening, Sam? Any time after I've had my supper. I need your help in sorting it all out." Sam was still reluctant but he agreed.

There were two more calls to be made. Near the Council offices was a large public car park. Richard left the Fiesta and crossed to the private parking area for Staff Cars. Each space was labelled 'Chief Executive', 'Environmental Health Officer', 'Chief Planning Officer'. One space was marked Parks Superintendent. It was occupied by a dark green Volvo Estate.

It was only a few yards to the office of the local evening paper. They obligingly produced the files for January. Each issue carried the Radio and Television programmes on the centre pages. On the evening of 21st January 'Dad's Army' had begun at 10.00 and finished at 10.30 pm.

Chapter 26

There was a much greater choice of meals in Richard's deep-freeze than there had been in the old days. That evening however, he was not hungry. He prepared baked beans on toast and forced himself to eat. Afterwards, he drank more cups of strong coffee than was usual. He watched the television news and was quite indifferent to the sensational arrest of a serial killer. For the first time, crime had no interest for him.

After his supper he took out the notes he had so carefully made. If he was right — if he was right — two men with blood on their hands were going to be ruined and their wives and children's lives shattered too. How could men like Polk face situations like that every day of their lives? How could he live with that knowledge afterwards? He remembered a game that he had once played at a children's party. Was it called 'murder'? You had to guess who the murderer was after sitting in the dark. Something like that he recalled. Now it was as if the game had become real and instead of a child pretending to be dead there was a real victim bleeding on the carpet.

Sam came round at eight o-clock. He refused tea, coffee or a soft drink and sat silently with an obstinate expression on his face. When he did speak, he was not encouraging. "Yes, they did it but there's still no real proof." Richard picked up his notes. "Now listen Sam. Let me go through it from the beginning."

"The motive I think, was sure from the beginning. It was something to do with the Colonel's work on the Council. At first, I thought it was some other Council member who was opposed to his views. I wasted a lot of time looking for someone like that and made myself unpopular with my policeman friend. It was nonsense anyway. Local Councillors are not the sort of people to do murders. I never thought it possible that people might kill in order to save their jobs."

"Then we worked out how the body got into the park. Finding that bit of lino under the hedge told us how they hid it. You worked that out for yourself. Then, we found out where the lino came from. Again it pointed to the Council where there were two men, both with serious family problems who faced redundancy and loss of income because of the policies that the Council Chairman was pressing for. There was to be a meeting of a Special Committee to make a decision in a week or so. They had to act quickly."

"You said there was a letter to get him on the train?"

"That was easy for them. His stockbroker had done some business for the Staff Investment Club. They would have been able to get hold of a sheet of their office stationary and make a photocopy. It would deceive the Colonel whose eyesight wasn't too good anyway. He would have put the letter away in his inside pocket but they would have retrieved and destroyed it. Got rid of any 'incriminating evidence'. "

"Yes, I follow that so far but why did they need to get him on that train? It would mean that no-one would miss him for the next twelve hours. They might even have known that he sometimes stayed at his club, but I don't think that likely."

"How did they get him off the train?"

"That was easy. One of the two and I think I know which one, — was at Bridgeminster station to see him get on the train. His wife saw someone she thought she recognised when she dropped him off. The other one was already at Bushwell station, probably standing by the public phonebox, waiting for a message telling him that the Colonel was on the train and which carriage he was in. Come to think of it, they may have had car phones. The train takes about ten minutes to get to Bushwell. Your friend Buckridge says there was someone pacing up and down the platform outside the sheltered area. He wouldn't want to be recognised. When the train came, he got on and persuaded the Colonel to get off."

"How could he do that?"

"He must have thought up a story. He knew that the reason for the Colonel's journey wasn't urgent business. He'd say that there was some important decision to be made that had cropped up which needed the Chairman's approval. Something to do with the Housing Department probably."

"He'd have had a car ready: no it must have been one of the Council's vans. He would then have driven Wainwright to some quiet place. The Grendon estate would be just the right spot. Not many people about in the daytime. He would have known that two of the houses were empty and he would have the keys."

"The roll of lino was already stored in that old shed. They should have noticed that the edges of it were old and liable to crumble. I think he may have been killed as he entered the house and left there until the evening. The killer probably waited in the house until he saw Mrs Mannheim opposite leave her home to go shopping. Then he drove away in the van."

"They both came back in the evening in an estate car. Mrs Mannheim saw it parked before she turned in. I checked the T.V. programme, 'Dad's Army' was on, on the night of 21st January."

"What happened next?"

"They hid the body inside the roll of lino and reached the Abbey Gardens sometime before midnight. If anyone had seen them they would have only have suspected them of dumping rubbish illegally by the bottle bank."

"Why put it in the park?"

"To give them more time. If they'd left the body anywhere else it might have been discovered that night."

"Could they have got that roll with the body in it over the wall? Heavy."

"Easy. They could put it on the top of the bottle bank, and then onto the roof of the little toolshed and so, into the park."

"The shed's not by the bottle bank."

"The bottle bank is on wheels so they only had to move it a few yards. Another bit of lino broke off as they got it over the wall. They moved the bottle bank back and left the roll beside it where your lads found it!"

"Why all the bother? Why didn't they go in through the park gates?"

"Three reasons. Firstly, Henry Marder's lodge is right by the gates. Secondly, the gates are heavy and would make quite a noise when opened. Thirdly, there were only two keys. If there was evidence that the gates were used it would point to someone in the office where the spare key was kept. Doing it that way would remove suspicion from someone who had the key."

"It was risky putting him over the wall."

"Not all that. There is only one street lamp in that bit of road. The police don't walk the beat all night nowadays. The whole job took only three or four minutes."

"There's not much evidence is there?"

"Well, we've got the pieces of lino and there's Mrs Mannheim. She saw the Council van with two men leaving it. One large and the other small. Colonel Wainwright was small. She saw the estate car that night. Garrowby has a 'Y' registered Volvo Estate."

Sam leaned back in his chair to consider all this. "If it was a Council van the journey has to be logged and the mileage recorded."

"Not a problem for the Head of Department. It will be properly recorded you see."

Sam had run out of questions and Richard went to the sideboard and poured himself a drink. Sam accepted an orange juice from a cardboard packet and they sat sipping.

"There's one thing you've forgotten," he said. "She said that van was green. All the Council vans are red with a yellow badge on the side."

"All of them?"

"There's only six or seven of the small ones. They've got bigger ones and lorries. They're red too."

"She could have been mistaken."

"It's a bright sort of red." Richard paused. He remembered the widow's words. She had said that the van was green.

"You're right Sam. She said it was green. I've just remembered that she said the estate car was red. Garrowby's Volvo is dark green!"

"She wouldn't be wrong about both?"

"No, I suppose she wouldn't be." There was another long, silence. Richard's gaze wandered around his fairly tidy sitting room. The floral curtains his mother had chosen for him, the carpet brought down from his old room after she had died, the familiar books on the shelves.

He got to his feet. From the shelf he took the volume of Eliot's poetry, a prize for English Literature in the Lower Sixth, bound in dark green leather and the small red volume of Milton's 'Comus', a work which had given him much trouble when doing his 'A' Levels.

"Sam," he said, holding the two books, "Did you notice anything strange about Mrs Mannheim's room?"

"Not especially. Funny taste though. My Emma wouldn't have liked those curtains."

"Anything else? What did she have on the table?"

"One of those knitting machines? I gave Emma one for her birthday three years ago but she couldn't get on with it! Gave it to Helen in the end."

"What was she making?"

"Some sort of woolly thing — a jumper?"

"Did you notice anything about it?"

"Not really: funny choice of colours too, though. Didn't seem to match!"

"Do you see what I'm driving at?"

Sam did not take long to work it out.

"Red and green — you mean she could be colour blind? We've got a driver on the carts like that. Said he wouldn't know 'Stop' from 'Go' if it wasn't on the top! I read somewhere that lots of people suffer from it."

"Exactly. Come on, we need to make a quick call on Mrs Mannheim!"

Sam though, had had enough for one day. "You'd better go without me Sir. I've got my bike. I'll be getting home to shut up my pigeons. Big race on Saturday."

Richard was beginning to learn that Sam was a man not easily persuaded. He let the dustman out and got into the car. He put two books in his pocket and drove to the Grendon Estate.

Chapter 27

Although it was getting dark, there were still children playing in the road. 'Pop' music sounded deafeningly from the house next door to the widow's.

"Oh Sir Richard, do come in! Is it about the bungalow?"

"I'm afraid I haven't been able to do anything about that yet, Mrs Mannheim. There's just one thing I wanted to ask you about: the matter we discussed this morning. It's rather a personal question I'm afraid. I hope you won't mind."

Richard followed her into her immaculate sitting room. This time 'Tibbles' came and sniffed at his shoes. "There, he's going to be friendly. Don't stroke him though, Sir Richard. He does scratch at times."

"Mrs Mannheim, — what I wanted to ask you was — what colour is this book?" Mrs Mannheim blushed. "Oh dear, why I'm sorry but I can't — how did you know?" The lady looked on the point of tears. "I've always been like that. I wanted to be in the Wrens like my sister, but they wouldn't accept me so I stayed on the farm."

"You are colour blind?"

"Yes they gave me a book with coloured letters in it and I couldn't read them but my eyesight is very good for my age. I only wear glasses when I read the newspaper. The doctor said I was the only girl he'd ever had with it."

"Please don't worry about it. I'm very sorry to have to ask you. It was because of something you said this morning." Richard did not want to explain the reason for his question and diverted the conversation to Mrs Mannheim's housing problems. She appeared to be satisfied. Obviously she expected that a titled gentleman, who was in some vague way connected with the Council, would ask inexplicable questions! In any case, her mind was firmly fixed on bungalows!

The reaction came when he got home. He sat with his second drink and tried to collect his thoughts. He had been meddling with things that did not concern him. Surely the police would have discovered the killers in the end? Now he would have to do something: lives were going to be ruined. Garrowby had an invalid wife. Henshaw had been married and there might be children. He couldn't pretend that he had been motivated by a sense of public duty. Even the Colonel's widow had not been concerned that the killers should be punished. Twice he got out of his chair to phone Polk and twice changed his mind. Instead he made a long distance call.

It was fifty miles to the unlovely industrial town where Father Randall had his Parish but next morning the old Fiesta covered it in less than an hour and a half.

It was a bright early summer morning when Richard drove up the neglected driveway of the drab red-brick, late Victorian Vicarage next to the even more depressing Gothic revival church. Building workers were removing the last of the scaffolding from the roof which Richard's money had restored.

Richard had had very little to do with priests. There had been a curate who had conducted his confirmation classes. (His mother had insisted on him being 'done'.) His strange manner with adolescent boys had much puzzled him at the time. There had of course, been many ordinands at Oxford. They had seemed to drink rather more than others and to tell cruder stories but he had never brought his problems to any churchman. They would probably want to discuss his soul. Hadn't someone said that 'all conflicts are theological'? The trouble was, he did not really believe in Theology. He supposed that Father Randall being 'High', often heard confessions. It was also fashionable today to go for 'counselling'. Perhaps the two things were much the same.

Father Randall had just returned to the vicarage after his morning Celebration. He called it Mass, Richard remembered. He was eating a boiled egg in his untidy kitchen and invited his visitor to sit down with him and drink coffee.

Father Randall did indeed have much experience of 'counselling'. Most of his penitents were widows or maiden ladies and their problems often lay in their sexual and other repressions. Through his experience therefore, the vicar knew enough about human nature to recognise the deep distress of his visitor. His normal lighthearted, slightly cynical attitude disappeared.

"I encouraged you in this work," he murmured as he listened. "I have a duty to help you." He sat silently as Richard poured out his story, the tips of his fingers pressed together almost as though in prayer.

"Don't tell me though, to do what my conscience dictates. It is not that I think I have done wrong. I suppose in a sense it is right to uncover a crime and see that justice is done. It's just that it's not like it is in the detective stories. Perhaps I am not strong enough. I keep feeling sorry for them."

"You are right to feel sorry."

"What am I to do then?"

It was some time before the priest replied. "I have never been asked a question like that. Most of my people bring me more straightforward problems. I don't know that I am any better qualified to advise you than your dustman friend."

"Perhaps; — if you feel brave enough — you would have to be very brave....you should go and see these men you suspect. It is only suspicion after all. Let them have the chance to give themselves up. As I say, it would take great moral courage and perhaps physical. They might be dangerous if they are desperate."

Richard paled. "I had thought of that but ......"

"It would be very hard and I wouldn't blame you if you left it all to the police. You will have to tell them very soon in any case."

There was little more to say. Richard took his leave after being shown the completed work on the church roof and then drove more slowly on his return trip to Bridgeminster. He lunched with small appetite at a 'Little Chef' and got home in the early afternoon. It took him three more hours to make up his mind.

Chapter 28

The house in Curtis Avenue was a semi-detached with bay windows. The small front garden looked neglected and the dark green Volvo was parked in front of the open garage door.

It seemed to Richard that it needed a supreme effort to press the bell knob. He was feeling very weak and frightened. The sound of a cheerful series of notes on distant tubular chimes was incongruous.

Garrowby opened the door. Richard realised with surprise that he had seen the man somewhere before. He was tall, over six feet and remarkably thin. His high forehead and receding hair made him look more like an ageing academic than a horticulturist. Sam had said that he was in his fifties but he looked older. He spoke in a quiet voice but only one word, "Yes?"

"Mr Garrowby, I presume?" It sounded banal. "My name is Smith, Richard Smith. May I come in? I have something rather important to say to you."

"Smith? Richard Smith? Sir Richard isn't it? I've heard of you. You're standing for the Council are you not? Is it something to do with the Council? Wouldn't it be better to deal with it in office hours, if it is?"

"No it's not Council business; not exactly."

Garrowby led him into a sitting room not unlike Richard's own. It had obviously lacked a woman's touch for some time.

"My wife's been ill. She only gets up for an hour or two in the afternoon when the District Nurse comes. I may have to go up if she rings."

Richard murmured something in sympathy. Garrowby indicated a chair and sat opposite to Richard with his back to the window.

The bright evening sunlight made his face difficult to see.

"If it's anything to do with the election I'm afraid I can't help you. I'm a Council employee and I couldn't do canvassing or anything like that. In fact, I'm not at all political, you know."

"It's nothing to do with that. I have to tell you something which you may find disturbing. If I have made a mistake I will owe you a deep apology."

"An apology? But I've never even met you before." The man's face showed no expression and his voice did not falter.

"I want to tell you a story. It's about the death of Colonel Wainwright, the former Chairman of the Council."

"That was last winter."

"Yes. You mustn't think I am a detective or in any way connected with the police. But I got interested in the case. You see I retired from work after I inherited —"

"Yes, I heard."

"Well, I've been looking into the case in a rather amateurish sort of way. Yesterday, I found the last piece of evidence. I think I know why the murder was done and who did it."

"Shouldn't you go to the police?"

"I shall, but I thought I should speak to you first."

"Because the body was found in the park?"

"No. Let me tell you what I believe."

"The murder was committed by two men, both of them Council employees. Both of them were threatened by the Colonel's policy of cutting Council costs by combining departments and making staff redundant. They both had serious personal commitments and feared the loss of their positions. One of them at least, was of an age when it would not be easy to find another job."

Garrowby appeared unmoved. Richard felt that he had possibly expected this visit and was prepared for it.

"These two men must have planned the murder. They faked a letter which induced the Colonel to get on a London train. At the first station, one of them boarded it and persuaded their victim to get off. He told the Colonel some story to convince him that he was needed for important Council business. The other man had phoned his fellow conspirator from Bridgeminster station to confirm that their victim had got on the train. I think that the Colonel's wife caught a glimpse of the man but not clearly enough to identify him."

Had Garrowby's face showed a trace of relief? It was hard to say. "The man at Bushwell drove the Colonel to the Grendon housing estate — what was once the old airfield. There are two empty houses there, a little way away from the other dwellings. I think that the Colonel was killed there, most probably as he entered the house and his body left there for the rest of the day."

"Later that day, both the men came to the house. Some days before, they had placed a roll of old lino from the Council offices in the rickety garden shed. They placed the body in the roll and put it in the back of an estate-type vehicle. They left, probably around midnight and drove to the road that runs round the south side of the Abbey Gardens — you know the spot?"

Garrowby nodded. "I was puzzled as to how they got it over the wall. There was a small tool shed built against the fence. If they moved the bottle bank a few yards they would have been able to get over. They left it on the gravel path where the park keeper found it the next morning. The snow had gone and there would be no footmarks."

"I found a piece of brown lino by the fence and another very small piece in the shed at the Grendon Council house. They left the roll of lino by the bottle bank after returning it to its original position. The dustmen removed it the next day."

"Why are you telling me all this?"

"Because you are tall and thin. Because your job was threatened by Colonel Wainwright's plans and because a resident of the Grendon estate says she saw a dark red Volvo Estate car, outside the house where I believe, the murder took place."

"I have a green Volvo." The voice was still without emotion.

"I forgot to tell you, the witness is colour blind. People with that handicap see green as red."

There was a long silence. Eventually the man spoke.

"Sir Richard, I see what you are getting at. I hope you have not made these suggestions to any other person. Slander is a very serious matter. You are a rich man I believe but even you would find the damages very heavy."

"I thought you might take it like that. I have said all that I want to say now. I will do nothing more in the matter for the next twenty four hours: then I must talk to the police."

"I understood that the police had dropped the case."

"I don't think that they ever drop murder cases. Goodbye, Mr Garrowby."

The Parks Superintendent showed him out but apart from a threat of an action for slander he had showed little emotion: not even much interest.

As Richard drove away, a thought occurred to him. When he reached the main road, he drove a few yards and then turned into a lay-by where during the day a small canteen provided lorry drivers with well-earned hot, strong, cups of tea. He switched off the engine and waited. Ten minutes later, the green Volvo emerged from Curtis Avenue and drove at high speed towards the city. It was seven thirty pm.

Chapter 29

It was Mrs Sellers who saved Richard's life and the lives of the other inhabitants of the flats. Afterwards, she explained that she could not sleep that night and so she got up to make herself some hot milk.

She smelt burning and opened her door. Her screams raised the alarm. The fire engine arrived within minutes. The remains of two plastic jerry cans which had contained petrol, were found at the foot of the staircase. Waste paper and old rags had also been used. The entrance hall was burned out and Richard's door was warped and blistered.

Inspector Morris spent the morning with one of the fire officers, looking for clues. It was a clearly an arson attempt. He questioned Richard. "Was there anyone with a grudge against you Sir? A former pupil perhaps: we had a case like that once." Richard denied the possibility and asked after Sergeant Polk. "He's dealing with a nasty little case on the other side of the city but I'll tell him you were asking after him."

The flat smelt abominably but the phone was still working. It was necessary to be extravagant and Richard rang the Angel Hotel and asked if they could put him up. It might be some time before his flat was habitable, he explained so could they let him have a bedroom and a sitting room?

They promised him the 'honeymoon suite'.

"Was Sir Richard .....?"

"No, Sir Richard was not." He would arrive in time for lunch and would they keep him a table? Richard packed enough clothes for four or five days and drove to the Angel. The hotel was once a coaching inn and the garage was reached through an archway. Here, the stagecoaches used to change their horses in times gone by. Across the green, the cathedral bells were ringing a marriage peal. The Evangelical Bishop was for once, reluctantly wearing a cope, in which to conduct the wedding of the eldest son of the Earl of Bridgeminster to a well-known television actress whose charms had been frequently displayed on page four of one of the more popular papers!

The hotel bar was full of reporters and photographers, waiting for the Bishop to finish his tedious homily, before they could dash across the Green to get their pictures.

Richard ate his steak and kidney pie followed by apple tart. The 'Angel' prided itself on its good plain English cooking. After lunch, he retired to his sitting room. They had clearly found it difficult to get honeymoon out of their minds. Both rooms were full of expensive flowers and a heart-shaped box of chocolates stood on the side table. There was also however, a large television set. Richard wondered if honeymooners were likely to want to watch television! His mind dwelt on such things for some time: he even tried one of the chocolates. Then he sat in an easy chair and watched an old American film for the whole of the afternoon.

At four thirty, he rang the bell and asked for tea. Once or twice he looked carefully out of the window but saw no one he recognised in the street. He ordered an early dinner and looked for the telephone. It was in the bedroom on a table next to the very large bed, a special hand-set in a delicate pink decorated with rosebuds. Richard wondered if people on honeymoon ever phone from their bedside?! He picked up the phone and dialled the police station.

Sergeant Polk was in his office. He sounded tired. Richard explained that he was not at his flat and would Polk come round to see him at the Angel that evening. About eight o-clock perhaps? Polk had heard of the arson attempt and was duly sympathetic. He'd had a hard day; would tomorrow morning do? It took a great deal of persuasion to get the Sergeant to agree to come. Next, Richard dialled Sam's number and asked 'my Emma' to get her husband to come to the 'Angel' at eight o-clock. He would arrange for a taxi to collect him. She sounded wary and Richard guessed that her husband had hinted to her that there was some trouble brewing.

The maid brought the tea and a dinner menu. He would eat at seven, he told her and would she please also remember to send up a bottle of the Macallan whisky and a jug of fresh orange juice with three glasses? The girl looked disapproving but made a note of his order. He settled in his chair. It was five fifteen. He had not brought anything to read with him, so resorted to viewing children's television until the News at Six o-clock. He then took a bath in the 'en suite facilities'. He kept the door to the corridor locked.

Few guests at 'The Angel' dress for dinner. Richard put on a clean shirt and his blazer with his college badge. He toyed with the 'Pate Maison' but quite enjoyed the chef's attempt at 'Coq au Vin'. He allowed himself a half bottle of the hotel's overpriced 'house wine' but resisted the temptation to take a liqueur with his coffee.

The 'sweets from the trolley' looked unpleasant and he settled for a rather dried-up portion of Stilton. At seven forty five, he left his table and retired to his room .

Sam arrived first. "I've asked Detective Sergeant Polk to come as well. I want you to tell him what you know." Sam looked uneasy. He was probably the most law-abiding citizen of Bridgeminster but his world had always regarded the police with suspicion. They talked about the weather and Sam's pigeons but the dustman remained ill at ease. By the time James Polk arrived they were both sitting in silence.

Chapter 30

Polk was both tired and in a bad temper. He accepted a large helping of the Macallan and looked round the room appreciatively. "Just like a high-class brothel," was his comment. "Just right for honeymoons." Polk did not have any experience of such establishments. The ladies of Bridgeminster who followed the oldest profession occupied far humbler premises. Polk looked hard at the two others: neither of them looked in the mood for ribald jokes.

"Well, what's all this about then? Caught another burglar?! I've had a long hard day, so make it short and don't tell me about that bit of arson either. The Inspector's dealing with that. He's sure it was one of your former pupils. Might be that lad Gary you helped to nobble. Come to think of it, I'd have liked to burn half the teachers we had at my old school! Mind you, we don't get much of that sort of thing in Bridgeminster. We'll get them."

Richard took his sheaf of notes from his breast pocket with the two envelopes containing the fragments of lino. "Not more matchsticks?" Polk quipped. "Just listen Jim will you for a few minutes? I — we, — think we have worked out the solution to the Abbey Park murder."

"Oh God, not again. We've been through all that. The trouble I had ...."

"Yes, I know but just listen." Glancing at his notes from time to time, Richard gave the detective the history of his investigations. "It was all a question of finding a motive. The method was simple. Anyone might have done it but in this case it was 'when you know why, you know who.'"

"You thought it was one of the other Councillors."

"I was wrong. There were other people who were threatened by the Colonel's campaigning."

"I don't see it."

"I told you that money was at the root of the problem? Well money doesn't only come in coins and notes."

"What do you mean?"

"It comes in the form of a monthly pay cheque or a bank credit, a car mileage allowance and other perks. Policemen used to receive a 'boot' allowance didn't they?"

"I'm not with you."

"There was a Committee set up to consider the reorganisation of the Council departments. The Colonel was the Chairman and the Committee was considering merging two departments."

"So what? They're always doing that sort of thing. Same in the Force."

"It would mean, in this case, that two senior men would lose their positions and face redundancy."

"Happens every day."

"Yes, but let me tell you just who they were. The first was the Head of Housing."

"Who's he?"

"His name's Henshaw."

"Yes, I know him. Big chap isn't he? He was up on a drink-driving charge three or four years ago. Nothing against him otherwise."

"He had domestic problems, (divorce and so on), and his position would make the loss of his job more serious." Polk was listening now but still sceptical. Richard went through the evidence again. "The roll of linoleum, the Council house on the Grendon estate, the big man on the station at Bushwell, the tall thin man seen by Mrs Wainwright at Bridgeminster station, the evidence of the colour-blind Mrs Mannheim ....." Polk heard it all in silence.

"Well," he said, "It does sort of hold together but you'd never be able to convict someone on that sort of evidence. Not reasonable suspicion, for an arrest. By the way, you also said there were two of them. Who was your second suspect?"

"The Head of the Parks Department. A man called Garrowby. Thin and tall. I think you ought to talk to him too."

Polk's manner changed and he stared at Richard for a long moment. Eventually he spoke. "I can't do that!"

"Why not?"

"I told you that I'd had a long day. He's dead."

"Dead?!"

"Found in the kitchen of his house. A pipe from the car outside through the cat-flap and the whole house full of fumes. Sometime this morning."

"What about his wife?"

"They managed to bring her round. Postman spotted the pipe and forced his way in. She's in hospital. Cat survived too."

"What about Henshaw?"

"I wouldn't know. Where's the phone in this knocking-shop?" Polk went into the bedroom and could be heard talking rapidly. When he returned he seemed pleased with himself.

"I've got on to the Super' and he thinks there may be something in it. I'd better get back to the station. I must admit all this may do me a bit of good!" Polk made his way towards the door. "I suppose a man in your position won't want your share in it known to the papers? Or you Sam?"

Sam looked horrified at the very thought. Polk looked pleased.

"One of them must have been behind that bit of arson at your flat. Silly thing to have done of course. We'd have bound to get on to them after that. I always said it was a straightforward case!"

Richard and Sam were left alone. Sam had had enough!

Epilogue

Henshaw was arrested at Dover, when he was about to board a ferry. He blustered at first but soon cracked under questioning. As Polk said later he didn't have the spirit of a proper murderer. The police had found a Garage in Portborough which had sold a man four gallons of petrol in plastic cans on the night of the arson attack.

Richard's hope that his part in the affair would be kept secret were soon dashed. Oddly enough the fault was Emma Absey's. She told her friend Mary Bunting at a meeting of the United Reformed Church Ladies Guild, — in the strictest confidence of course. Mary told her husband, who then passed on what he heard, until the story reached the ears of Henry Collins, a freelance journalist and writer of romantic fiction under the pseudonym, Rosalind Pashley. It was the best scoop of his career for which he was well paid.

Richard, back in his refurbished flat, was besieged by reporters. The popular papers bore headlines about the 'Millionaire Baronet-Sleuth'. It was intolerable!

Flight was impossible as the election for Bridgeminster South were due in less than a week. Mrs Oldrieve too, was a source of trouble to him. She made him go canvassing and he had several unpleasant encounters with large dogs and one almost-violent affair with a very angry voter who blamed the Conservatives for the price of beer, the failure of his car to pass the MOT test and the break-up of his marriage!

The day of the election was rainy. Fewer than half the voters on the South Ward got to the Polls. At nine pm the count began and Richard watched with fascination as the little piles of ballot papers grew under the watchful eyes of the candidates and their supporters! At twelve minutes past ten precisely, the Returning Officer announced the result. Adrian South, Liberal Democrat, (and also Vegetarian, Friend of the Earth and former Nuclear Disarmer), had won by forty six votes. Richard did not ask for a re-count!

It was a further ten days before he felt he could get away. There were court proceedings to attend.

A travel programme on the television tempted him to try the Loire Valley. He had always liked Rabelais. He could take the car and wander about. He had never driven on the right-hand side of the road before but no doubt it could be attempted by easy stages.

Before he left the country he visited his solicitors. Mrs Mannheim was to be found a bungalow of her choice to be hers for life at a peppercorn rent. The lawyers were also to investigate Mrs Garrowby's circumstances and arrange for her to enter a private nursing-home and also to see what could be done for the various dependents of Mr Henshaw. Richard hoped that Father Randall would approve.

The day before his departure Richard received a visit from James Polk. His promotion to Inspector had come through and he had been celebrating. The Chief Constable had congratulated him on the way he had cleared up the Abbey Park murder. The man was pleased with himself but determined to be fair-minded. As he sipped a weak whisky and water which Richard had doubtfully poured him, he acknowledged his debt. "I don't mind telling you, Richard," he said, "You did give us some very useful tips!"

The next day Richard left England. It was not until the ferry was approaching Cherbourg that he remembered that he ought really to have done something about the Garrowbys' cat!